MW01703457

MONSTER'S ENEMY

BLACKTHORN ACADEMY FOR SUPERNATURALS

BOOK FOUR

CARA NORTH

NAUGHTY NIGHTS PRESS LLC• CANADA

MONSTER'S ENEMY

BLACKTHORN ACADEMY FOR SUPERNATURALS

BOOK FOUR

ISBNS: 978-1-77357-579-7

978-1-77357-580-3

PUBLISHED BY NAUGHTY NIGHTS PRESS LLC

EDITED BY: MICHELLE'S EDITS

COVER ART BY SILVANA G. SÁNCHEZ

@ SELFPUB DESIGNS

MONSTER'S ENEMY

He's in love with the one witch who could destroy them all.

Attending Blackthorn Academy has always been a dream to the Earth-borne witch with basic powers. When the invitation arrives, she can't wait to get to the place where so many of her ancestors thrived. Only, she arrived a week early, her magic is on the fritz, and her father tampered with her transcripts so she has to find a tutor to survive the Defense Against the Dark Arts class, and fast.

Brazrathan Patrick has shifted his focus to becoming a scholar. He stopped goofing around with his best buds and fellow monsters. Even stopped playing in the monster games as part of the team. Nothing would derail him from becoming the future valedictorian of his class and residential professor at this very school some day.

When the Headmistress throws curiosity to the wind, fate intervenes and brings two unlikely partners together. There are very few things that can kill a monster of Brazrothan's genealogical make-up, but the woman he loves might just be number one.

Monster's Enemy is book four in the Blackthorn Academy for Supernaturals shared world, featuring a curvy, kickass witch, a broody, half-gargoyle, half-demon, self-proclaimed loner, and more.

CHAPTER ONE

Eleanor

NERVOUS? WHO WOULD be nervous? Excited? Yes. That is the proper word for what I was feeling. Surely, I had no reason to be nervous on my first day. Especially because I would be a week early. Sometimes having my family name worked in my favor. As one in a long line of Easternwind witches who had attended the Blackthorn Academy, I practically grew up there. Well, in my mind, I practically grew up there. My grandmother on my father's side and aunts all told tales of their adventures. I could not wait to begin mine!

Which is exactly how I ended up here a week earlier than I was supposed to. I had been a bit too anxious and found myself on a transport with a handful of senior faculty and a few administrative staff members. I knew this because they greeted one another and asked questions. I experienced a few raised brows, a couple smiles, and a handful of hellos.

I remained quiet for the majority of the trip, but *I* knew *they* knew I was not one of them. I grew up in the *human* slash *mortal* slash *whatever they wanted to call it these days* "realm" with visits to my father's family in the parallel paranormal universe filled with magic, fantastical creatures and beings, and... everything I ever wanted.

My life was split between being overtly typical in one realm (the magic one) and exceptionally interesting in another (the moral one). I obviously chose my path to my father's delight and my mother's dismay. I may have been a very basic witch with limited knowledge, but the academy faculty and staff must have seen something on my application that made them say yes. I cast my gaze downward and sighed. They may have seen my last name and thought they were getting someone a bit more exceptional in this realm.

In the human realm, my magic, what

limited skills I had such as moving things, making things, growing plants faster, etc. worked well. Since arriving here, the only thing I knew for sure that worked was the bag my Grandmother Eaternwind had given me for school. It could hold a small apartment worth of things, but I had only put my necessities as my father had already shipped my trunks. The main difference so far was this trip had been the first I had ever taken that actually felt like magic was on my side.

One very human trip to Ireland and a special ferry ride would transport me and the rest of the passengers to our destination. My father's family was located in parallel New York, New York so we always used the spelled airplane that would take a magical path that landed in the *other* New York. It was not called New York and it was still nowhere near the academy I longed to be a part of. This was my first trip beyond the East coast of the United States in either universe so my anxiety level probably made my aura visible to anyone who cared to see it.

"You're a bit early, Miss Easternwind," a female voice said as the sun began to descend below the horizon. The colors were mesmerizing and I had to consciously pull my attention from them as the mystical haze of the colorful yet somehow plain fog began to appear.

"I don't like to be late." It sounded lame to my own ears, but it was true. I hated to be late for anything and when counting on the mortal realm for accurate travel, well, I really dreaded it.

However, this trip had been exceptionally easy. The slight creak of the ferry combined with the gentle motion made by the gentle waves was making me feel a bit sleepy.

She nodded. "Well, good thing I'm arriving today then." She smiled. "I have your room assignment. I don't know if you will count yourself lucky or not, but you will only have one roommate, Miss Maxine Mayhem."

"Mayhem?" I could feel my eyes widen at the last name. Okay, my last name is Easternwind which was because of the compass location my father's family had settled in and the fashion boutiques they established in both realms which made them a household name to wealthy patrons and centuries of fortune. What would cause someone to be named

Mayhem?

The woman who I still didn't have a name for said after a giggle, "She will be delightful. Don't judge a name by its connotation, right?"

I cleared my throat and shook my head. Then, as I felt the heat creep across my cheeks, I asked, "And your name is?"

She looked beyond me and said, "You can see the shore."

I turned to look and saw nothing but the dense fog. When I turned back to get her name, she was gone. I looked at the older merman settling into that spot and asked, "Did you see where she went?"

His brow went up. His pale-blue skin did nothing to hide his expression of amusement as he asked, "Who?"

Right. I smiled and shook my head.

"I." I cleared my throat and looked back toward the direction she indicated and immediately forgot my concern as she was right. I could see the shore. "We're almost there!"

He chuckled and said, "Yes. First year?"

I nodded.

"I remember my first year." He smiled and looked toward the shore. "Did you know that Blackthorn Academy was one the Blackthorn family castle. In 1666, they it became an institution for higher learning. If you flew over the top, it would look like a pentacle."

I listened to him reminisce with awe.

"When I was younger, they just installed the plumbing!" He laughed. "So glad they installed the plumbing. It's quite a hospitable facility now.

Everything you need. I live there full-time now. Blackthorn felt like home when I first stepped onto the grounds. After years of fighting it, I came back to teach and… well, it has been my home ever since."

"Wow." I looked at him and he smiled. Pleased with my reaction, maybe?

He nodded. "I also arrived early my first year."

My lungs seized at the thought. Then he nodded toward the destination and I forgot all about that frightful thought. I was too excited to finally see it. Any part of it. I maintained my barely-leashed composure as much as I could. I knew we were a ways from the school still but who cares? I was here. Almost on the island that would solidify my place in this realm when I graduated with a degree in the defensive arts and worked anywhere but in retail!

The rest of the trip was filled with recognizable landmarks from stories I'd been told. I was the only one exhibiting the barely contained awe of everything around me, though the mysterious professor seemed to find joy in that.

I was positive that what seemed like endless flights of stairs to the freshmen female dorms would finally take care of what magical grandmother liked to call my 'extra.' Coming from a family of fashionistas on both sides of the universe, my aunts sometimes spent time in the mortal realm and worked at the shop where they could create other designs, had made me aware of how to dress to impress but it never impressed the women in my family that I 'took after my mother' who 'must have taken after someone on her family's side.'

I often wondered if that full figure is why such a man as my father would have married a non magical woman over a magical one. He always joked that she was magic, just not the kind his parents approved of. I'd never met anyone from my mother's side of the family. She said when she met my father, it was clear that she loved him and that was all that mattered. They were apparently very strict and did not approve of him regardless of his wealth and stature in the human realm. My mother was definitely human. There were only a few times I found her doing anything strange like sitting in the garden for hours, but she loved the plants and flowers, so one of the first things I had my magical grandmother teach me was to make those bloom.

These thoughts helped me get to the top of the stairs. Then I had the long stretch of hallway because the room I was assigned with just one roommate was at the very end. Like, the door was looking at me like it should have been a broom closet and that's why I was placed there.

Unlike me, the majority of the student body were not interested in a lonely start to the semester. No worries. I had friends. Thousands of them in the library. No harm getting a start to the readings. I was, after all, an Easternwind witch. This meant there were expectations. High expectations, if my grandmother's lecture was true.

If my father's family name meant I

had a high bar to reach for, my mother was the exact opposite. She expected me to take over the accounting for the Easternwind Boutique. My mother loved working there but she liked math and did all the accounting in the back. The non-magic blood was a grave concern to my father's family since I was their only child. At least until I hit puberty. Then, it was obvious I had that Easternwind magic running through my veins. Running slowly, but running nonetheless. My mother had my sister when I turned fourteen. She didn't seem to age like others, but again, she worked in the fashion industry and took exceptional care of herself. I wasn't sure why they waited to see what puberty held for me, but they did. So now, I had a six year old little sister and a four year old little brother growing up together and without me since I would be here, in the magic realm for college. Still far away from my family.

I was about to feel sad when I opened the door to my dorm room. Inside was relatively spacious. This was one of the two person rooms so it was not as large as the ones that held three to four people. I had heard about those from my grandmother and aunts who had attended before. I was the first to experience this room. I liked it. I really wished it had a bathroom attached, but everyone had the shared space for showers and toileting which was fortunately at this end of the hall.

I placed my backpack at the foot of my bed, the one closest to the window. I was certain my trunks would arrive early as well, but they were not in my room yet. If they were not here by nightfall, I would ask. I reached into my backpack, the gift given to me by my grandmother for its ability to store just about anything, and pulled out the suitcase that had my most essential items in it. My father had assured me that I could rely on the system. That was very likely the case—which meant my trunks would arrive on time, whereas I was here early.

I sighed. Nothing to do about it now. I had to take advantage of the fact that I was first in the room. I hung a few items in the wardrobe, placed a book on the nightstand, and finally, claiming the desk I wanted, I pulled out my favorite lamp and hooked it up. "There. That should do it."

Settled that I had at least unpacked a

bit, I headed out of the room and toward the library. I figured that would be open for the professors, so it should not be too difficult for me to slip in and become familiar with my second home. I planned to spend a considerable amount of time in that location despite having a desk in my room. The passageway was eerily quiet and I could see how the whole vibe might be different when filled with excited freshmen, like me. Located on the very top floor, we would be getting our steps in for sure. My room, located at the very end of the hallway, may prove to be either the best location or the worst. I considered this as I imagined the variety of students that may be bustling about this hallway next week.

Would they be welcoming? Would I? I tended to be a bit awkward in social settings, so that sometimes came off as snobby. I think that had to do with my heritage. My father's family was quite shocked when he married my ordinary mother, and once they knew I was of their stock, for lack of better phrasing on their part, I discovered a whole other side to them.

I reached the main floor and then headed down to the library. It seemed a bit odd to put the library underground, but I was so conditioned by the traditional city structures and life that I found the sound of my own shoes against the floor odd. Lonely. It was so quiet I was certain I could hear my thoughts echoing off the walls. Once I was underground, I realized there was more than just a library down here. The signs pointed in various directions indicating a weapons training facility, what essentially amounted to the athletic department which boasted additional signage for the pool and workout rooms, and then, the library.

Inside the climate controlled room, it seemed like the books were endless. I walked around a bit and noted the archives room and the sign that said off limits without permission. Boo. I walked through the stacks and wished I could just read them all.

I finally made my way to the section I was anxious to see. My father had written many books but they were not sold in mortal stores, so I rarely got to see them shelved anywhere other than his office in our home.

Excitedly, I found the location only to lose all of that energy when I realized the books were shelved higher than my current height and arm reach would allow. I looked up and down the aisle only to realize there was not a ladder or step stool here like there had been in the main section and upon entry.

I considered walking back to the front. I'd already had quite a trek just to get here, would have to climb all those stairs to get back to my room. I bit the corner of my lip, looked up to the ceiling and hoped that I would not get in trouble on my first day. Especially since it was before my first day of classes. I spoke the words quietly, which may have been why the order of the books moved a bit too drastically.

Huffing out a breath, I decided at least I could reach them on the bottom shelves. Now, I just had to find them again.

CHAPTER TWO

Brazrothan

AS ONE OF the only tutors for Defense Against the Dark Arts studies left this year, I knew I needed to get a head start on the curriculum. As a junior and double major in defense and offense studies, it had been a minute since I reviewed the freshman reading list. I was looking at the list and seeking anything new that had been added or anything I might want to refresh on at that basic level again when I heard something.

I placed the book back on the shelf and just in time to watch it disappear and then another book appear in its place. "Huh."

I moved, quietly, as the books in this section continued to relocate themselves without much sense to their organization. This led me to one row in these stacks where a voluptuous redhead was moving to her hands and knees as she grumbled and began crawling, *backward*, toward me.

I tilted my head and tried to listen. She was so caught up in her hunt for whatever she was looking for, she hadn't even sensed my presence. I, on the other hand, was becoming more acutely aware of her with each lift and lower of toes, knees, and hands on that floor.

Closer, I could hear her say, "Where are you? You should be here."

She was talking to the books, not me, of course.

"Dammit." She sat up, resting that full ass on her heels. "Okay, this time, I want it right here, okay?"

My brow quirked. My inner demon had lots to say about that statement, but I was not going to let those thoughts win. One aspect of my life, being part demon and part gargoyle, meant I was destined to be single forever. Most gargoyles wanted to be sure they also had gargoyle descendents since we were almost extinct by some standards and most demons just... wanted to have fun at this age, so... yeah. Solitary living provided lots of time for academic excellence and I was excellent at academics.

I was also excellent at using my gargoyle to my benefit, which is why when she turned slightly to look around before casting what I now realized was her second spell in the library, she didn't even seem to notice the new addition to the end of the aisle. That would be me in a statuesque form of my choosing. Well, apparently, my demon's choosing as I ended up squatting with my elbow on my knee and my chin perched precariously so that if she did not watch herself, when she resumed backing down that aisle, she would back right into my—

"Ouch!" she yelped as the very pointed tips of my horns poked her in the ass. She stood quickly and turned to look down at me. “You.” She pointed. “I can’t believe I forgot you were there.”

She touched the tip of one horn with a finger and said, “I wish you could help me. I can’t seem to get my spell to work in here the way it does in any other library.” She puffed out a breath. “This is so frustrating.”

I wished I were looking up so I could see her face. I was really glad she was not paying as close attention to me or she might realize it had been what felt like ages since someone... fondled my horns. Actually, I wasn’t sure anyone had touched them like she was now. As a man of stone, I was definitely feeling hard... everywhere.

“What in the world?” One of the librarians was a few rows over. “Who's here?"

"Shit." The beautiful horn fondler patted my head as though I were a pet of some sort before saying aloud in response to the librarian, "Me. I'm here. I... couldn't reach a book."

I heard her steps as she moved to the end of the stack and toward the librarian. I shook out of my current state of arousal and insanity and moved in the opposite direction.

My mind would not stop conjuring the image of her crawling backward toward me. My demon would not stop altering that image. I was practically in a confused daze as I exited the library thinking: *Who the hell is she and what in the hell possessed her to just... fondle me... a statue... anything like that?* My inner demon had all sorts of thoughts attempting to answer that question for me. It wasn't like I was separate from the demon and gargoyle sides of me, but I used them as my good and evil scale, and right now, since my gargoyle was all about more touching from that woman, this year was feeling like the perfect year for me to be a bit… wicked.

CHAPTER THREE

Eleanor

"NO, NO, NO. You do not understand." I was attempting to remain calm and not get animated though my body was experiencing a whole new level of anxiety as I attempted to explain why I should absolutely NOT be in an advanced placement class.

"Your father provided documentation

that places you in the advanced course, not the beginner. I'm sorry, but you have that credit on your incoming transcript, so you have to take the advanced class." The advisor was speaking to the paper and not me, so I focused and tried to cast in the seconds it took for his head to lift and his eyes to meet mine. He simply did some sort of hand motion and said, "Do not try that again. It is grounds for academic probation."

I gulped. It was a spell to erase that nonsense my father had sent them. Transcript for Defense Against the Dark Arts? When the hell did he teach me defensive tactics? He wrote multiple books on the topic, but I never learned any of it. I was struggling with what I did learn. It was so much easier to cast spells, use my magic back in the mortal realm. I didn't know why. Had assumed the exact opposite would be true, but here I was, getting a scolding and a warning for the second time since arriving.

I nodded and said, "I'm sorry. I just—"

"If you feel you are not up to par, then get a tutor. Review this document and sign here." The paper appeared on the counter in front of me. I didn't need to read it. I knew I would need the tutor. I scribbled my name and the document disappeared. "You have the reading list. I suggest you get started."

I mumbled and grumbled all the way back to my room. I barely acknowledged the students also climbing or descending the stairs, heading down their passageways toward the rooms. I just remained focused on my feet, the next step in front of me, and eventually, the long passageway to the end of the hall where my room door was wide open. My roommate was here!

I stepped into the space hoping to present a better attitude, but found a beautiful blonde haired beauty moving my stuff.

"Excuse me?" I was a barely contained bundle of aggravation at this point. Nothing was turning out the way I had planned since finding out I was accepted to this prestigious academy.

"Oh, hi. I'm—"

"Moving my things?" I asked with more disdain than I had planned. The fact that she practically oozed perfection from head to toe only fueled my anger more. I wasn't sure why other than the fact that she was clothed in my family's newest competition for magical boutique garments. I tried to rationalize that as I looked her over and allowed my day of frustration to unload on my roommate!

"I need—"

"You need to put that down. You need to leave everything of mine right where I placed it. You need—" She looked confused and then like she felt sorry for me. I understood why a moment later.

"Darling, what is going on there? I'm so sorry for her behavior." My father's voice came through as my new roommate looked from me to the bed where she apparently had placed something rather than removed it.

She looked at me, shook her head, and as she passed, she said, "This is going to be a very long year together."

I closed my eyes and let out a sigh. As

I looked around, I realized she hadn't even brought her stuff in.

"I sent this so we could communicate. Maxime was kind enough to bring it inside rather than leave me in the mail room since she was coming to your shared room." My father left no room for me to explain. "Why in the world would you be so rude to your roommate? Especially Maxine Mayhem. Do you have any idea how powerful her family is? What it took for me to ensure you would be roomed with someone—"

I sighed. I shook my head and could no longer hold the tears back. I picked up my father's communication device and moved to my closet where I placed it and shut the door to the sound of his warnings and disapproval of my behavior. I moved to my bed, dropped face first onto the mattress and pillows and began sobbing as quietly as I could. Maybe this was all wrong for a good reason. Maybe I didn't really belong here after all. My mother had a very good life as a plain human with an office and a job and... I sniffed. That wasn't the life for me, but maybe this wasn't going to be the answer I had hoped for either. I looked over to her desk and the only thing she had brought into the room other than the communication globe my father had sent, three letters addressed to her. She had simply brought up the mail. When I looked at my desk, I knew there was no room for what essentially was the size of a large fortune telling ball.

Maxine Mayhem returned and began unpacking her things in an orderly and silent fashion. She did not acknowledge me or my tears and for that, at least, I was grateful.

CHAPTER FOUR

Brazrothan

I LOOKED AT my tutoring schedule once more and then at the door. This Eleanor Easternwind should have already arrived. As a freshman in an advanced placement Defense Against the Dark Arts class, I was surprised she wanted to be tutored. Maybe that was a mistake, except I knew she had to sign that form on site after speaking to an academic advisor.

I considered the last name and the textbook in my hand and wondered if she needed more practical application rather than knowledge. Before I could stand, the door to the private room in the library opened and the beauty who backed into my horns stepped inside. She was breathing heavy, as though she had ran to this meeting, and the disheveled look of her had my entire core growing warm from the sight of pink cheeks, messy hair, and…

"I'm sorry I'm late." She leaned forward and placed her hands on her knees as she caught her breath. "I had to run. We can't use the mirrors to make the travel less. I'm all the way—"

I could feel the gruffness of my voice

before I said the first word, so I cleared my throat in an attempted to tamp down that desire. The sound caught her attention and the immediate worry evident from her frowning lips and scrunched brow had me speaking in a tone I was unaware I had. Gently, softly, I said. “Have a seat. We’ll spend this session getting to know more about what aspects of defensive arts you need help with.”

She gulped, nodded, and then moved to the seat across from me. She opened the flap on the shoulder bag and said, “At least this still works the way it is supposed to.”

She reached in and pulled out a copy of the same book I had in front of me.

I looked at the book her father had written and asked, “Are you having trouble with your magic?"

She nodded, snorted a sound that had me holding back a snicker as she flipped through the pages and said, "I've never read this book before. Could never get my hands on the ones my father had on his shelves. He's written several."

I'd read them all. "Yet you are in an advanced course."

She laughed and the sound and expression was so intense I knew before she said it what the problem was. "Exactly! How the hell does he think being his daughter is enough to make me advanced in all this? Like his bloodline was supposed to code my genetic magical makeup to just know things because he did. I know nothing!"

I started to speak, but she was not done venting.

As she pulled her auburn hair into a messy ponytail she continued, "And everything I did know, or thought I knew how to do is like..." She made a sound as she also moved her arms and hands about as if indicating trying to grasp at something in the air. "I can't catch one break. You know?"

I did not know. I nodded because I was growing more interested in this unusual witch with every word she spoke. When she stopped speaking, which was several minutes later, she looked at me as if really looking at me for the first time. Her eyes blinked and when she focused on my horns, I was sure she knew it was me she literally backed into in the library.

Instead, Eleanor said, "I don't mean to be rude, but I've never met anyone with your… features before."

Again, there were not a lot of students in the school in the past years. They had canceled more than one class due to low enrollment. Our realm was not exactly one where a college degree was needed, though it certainly helped, especially when traveling to or through other dimensions. There were only a handful of gargoyles around and most of them had shorter horns. The demon side of my line had huge horns, but demons could be horned or hornless, so even if I was small in the horn department, I made up for it in the rest of my body because gargoyles were known for the muscles, the endurance, and of course, the ability to turn to stone and perch for hours, days, months, years, eternity if from the right lineage. My horns were considered medium for a demon and large for a gargoyle of my age. “I’m… a demon.”

Not a lie, just not the whole truth.

She nodded. “Oh. Okay.” She looked at my eyes and her brow went up. She knew there was more, but was not going to ask. I was not going to tell her anyway.

“What?” I asked because she was still seemingly processing that information.

She gulped and I focused on her throat and my demon side began flashing all sorts of illicit images in my head. I looked at her lips as she said, “I just thought demons would be more… offense than defense.”

I smiled and nodded. “I double majored. It’s good to know both sides.”

She said, “Good point.” Then a

distinct sound disrupted her.

The blush of color heating her face made me want to smile, laugh, but I would not embarrass her further than she obviously already was.

"I—" she started.

"Have you been outside the cafeteria yet?" What the hell was I doing?

She shook her head.

My mouth was on autopilot. "Would you like to grab dinner in town then?" And before she could refuse or cause my face to heat with embarrassment, I added in a rush, "I already planned to go to the pub." She looked at the table between us. Now, I was the one who couldn't seem to shut up. "It's good food, but I understand if you'd rather—"

"I'd love to go." She closed the book in front of her and as she placed it back in her small bag, I tried to let out a quiet breath of relief.

Eleanor was not what I had expected. Her full, inviting lips seemed to never stop moving. She was curious about everything around us as though she only read about it in a book or something. I was drawn to her in ways I had never anticipated. It wasn't like I could find a mate the way others could, yet here I was, listening to this witch tell me about the flowers she was seeing along this ride to town as though she wanted my confirmation the information she was sharing was correct. And it had been, probably, I kept getting distracted, but what I tuned in to hear sounded accurate.

"You seem very fond of plants. Are you studying—"

"No." She laughed. "No way. I'm a... basic witch. Basic being the key term and witch being the goal. The degree should satisfy my father and his family that I can do more. Possibly... something other than manage a magical clothing store in this realm or a fancy boutique in the one I grew up in."

My brow shot up so far on my forehead I thought it would touch my hairline. "What realm are you from?"

She leaned in a bit and despite my best efforts, I let my eyes linger on the sight of the top of her left breast exposed by the angle.

After worrying a kissable bottom lip for a moment, she whispered, "The human realm. Planet Earth."

"At least you are not from Mars." I made my line of sight shift to her face.

"The only magical being I met from that planet was wild and crazy." She opened her eyes wide. I smiled and added, "Best roommate I ever had. Sophomore year."

She let out what could only be a breath of relief. She then said, "Please don't tell anyone else I'm... half... human."

I nodded. This was the moment I should tell her, but I couldn't. I didn't know this woman well enough to trust her with all my secrets. Only a handful of faculty and staff knew my origins. Instead of confessing my own mix of parentage, I blurted out, "Did you know the town's name is Wellspring because of the island's ability to create and provide its own fresh water sources?"

She nodded. "It's in the freshman orientation."

"Ah yes. Right." While there had been many opportunities in my young adult life to run wild and take advantage of the physical offerings by many in the academic setting, I had not. Not once. Not one. Had not even read a book about it beyond the basic anatomy and physiology of magical species and creatures. I wasn't sure if my unique design would even work with what she had over there. Essentially, a human body type.

"Pub or seafood?" she asked and I realized she may have been talking all this time, but I was staring straight ahead trying to figure out if I could find a way to know for sure before my mating alarm rang any louder in my ears. How? Why? This made no sense.

"Pub." I needed a drink and was old

enough to get one. She was too, but I definitely needed some liquid courage to settle myself down and really think about the consequences of what my body was telling me. Mine. She had to be mine. I had to have her. There was no other path in my current state of mind. Every moment I spent with her was like I fell deeper under her spell. Only, I knew she was not powerful in this realm and if she did cast a love spell on me, it would result in me falling for one of those plants and not her. She was not terribly good at getting what she wanted through her witchy powers yet. But that gave me an idea. "And then to Penhallows." And for good measure, "And Moonbright after that."

Yeah, I needed a couple pints. I'd known her less than a day and I was already in provider mode. I was already determined to do whatever it took to care for my mate. Mate. *Fuck*. Mate.

CHAPTER FIVE

Eleanor

IS IT EVEN possible to be more attracted to someone than I was to Braz. Braz. One more sip of this cherry beer and I might just call him that out loud. He had told me during our study session that most people called him Patrick as it was what everyone on the sporting teams did. Inside Buckingham's (Buckie's) Pub

& Billiards, Braz ate like a demon. I wasn't sure if he was eating so much because he was hungry or if it was to keep from sharing more about himself with me.

"Patrick!" An actual demon slapped him on the back and winked at me. "Introduce us to your new friend."

He didn't seem exceptionally thrilled to speak to them as he said, "This is Eleanor. Elanor, this is the... debate team?"

They roared with laughter. All of them. The beautiful blue skinned, blond haired creature that reminded me of a mermaid if they were guys, shoved at the demon's back and said, "Let's go! We have to get this done tonight."

"Later, Patrick." The demon and Braz did some sort of hand gesture and the team was heading out the door.

I waited, but Braz was not going to be forthcoming with the information, so I had to ask. "Are you on that team?"

"I used to be. Not anymore." He shrugged.

"Oh." I wanted to know more. He was not going to disclose more, so I opted for, "Does your skin turn a different color when you drink or—"

"What?" He looked at his arms, his hands.

I shook my head. "It's your neck. Somewhat... pink."

"Pink!" It was a statement not a question. He lifted his head back and pointed as he asked, "Where? Here? There?"

The more he talked, the more it spread to a deep magenta all over him. I gulped and admitted, "Well, now it is... everywhere."

He closed his eyes and when he opened them, I felt something akin to fear, but also... I was... curious.

"I can't believe this is happening to me." He shook his head. His long black hair seemed to move in slow motion like he had his own personal fan that displayed all of his sexy features to their best at this moment. Everything, absolutely everything he did was... turning me on.

"Me either." It was a breathy whisper and I squeezed my knees tighter together for both the sudden relief of friction and because I wanted to lock myself in place before I climbed over this table and attacked his lips with mine.

"We should go." He inhaled sharply

and I watched his nostrils flare. “Now.”

He called out, “Put it on my tab.”

One look at him and the server nodded, not coming near us. As we left the pub, he pulled his shirt over his head. Wowza. Mygowza. Sheeshyazowza. My brain was speaking awed nonsense as my eyes absorbed the awesome sight of him. Then they popped up, like bat wings extending from his back in one sharp motion. I gasped and the creature who was my defensive arts tutor looked at me as though I should run in another direction, but my feet were stupid, so they moved toward him instead. “You have wings.”

His transformation continued, only slightly altering his facial features to be a bit more rugged, a tad more carved in stone. His teeth were a bit sharper when he spoke and said, "We need to get back to the campus. Immediately."

I nodded and looked for the transportation that had brought us, but it was gone already. Before I could turn back to ask what the plan was, he had swooped me up, into his firm, strong arms as he pushed off the ground and... we were flying. Well, he was flying. I was trying not to choke him as I held on for my life. If he thought he would drop me like that eagle dropped a turtle in our backyard that one time, he was sorely mistaken. I was not about to let go and I doubted he would navigate as smoothly with me dangling from his neck like a necklace.

A few moments into the ride, I dared to open my eyes and pull my face away from the heat and safety of his chest.

"Where are we going?"

I could see the school ahead of us, but it didn't seem like he was about to land. Or at least not like I thought he would. What the hell did I know? I was basing all this on things I had seen or read and… oh. A specific passage in a book I read one summer at my magical grandmother's house popped into my mind. I remembered when I read it, I got all tingly and awkward. It called to me on some level and I was too young to understand why. He… was flushing in color because his… mate was near.

I didn't even hear his response. I closed my eyes and tucked my cheek to his chest and wished we never left campus. Wished I could understand why, the first time I was interested in a guy, he would be hit with the mating stick and need to get me out of his way as soon as physically possible.

CHAPTER SIX

Brazrothan

FUUUHHHCK. I WAS out of control. My body was reacting in ways my brain was not cool with, yet I could not deny the physical responses. They were instinctual and since I had absolutely zero practice hiding them since these were all knew to me, I was defenseless. Hell, I had no offense either. Why didn't I just go with the guys? I wouldn't be all lit up and agitated by the woman in my arms.

I landed on the top of the school's roof. There was a flat square space and it was hidden by the tall structures of the roof's aesthetic. I liked to come here and perch between two of the larger pillars, settle into my gargoyle completely and regroup.

I placed Eleanor on her feet and said, "I—"

"I'll see you in two days, right? Next session. I won't be late again. Don't worry." She headed in one direction and then the next as I processed the fact that she was leaving before I even had a chance to explain.

"The door is—"

"Right. I see it. Maybe I should find a

way to land on the roof more often. Closer to my floor." She was nervous and... oh shit. She may be scared of me.

I could feel a part of my heart break. I could feel that inner demon in me urge my feet forward. Trap her, keep her—but that would not prove that she was mine or safe. In fact, it would just make her more afraid and likely to agree to anything. My good and evil were warring inside my brain and I was like a third party tuning them out and dealing with the fact that my mate just shut the door and I could no longer see her.

I needed to see her. I considered this a long time. Long enough for my wings to settle, my color to return to normal, and my dick to remember how uncomfortable these clothes are if it is not relaxing.

I took in a deep breath and headed down the stairs. This entry took my mate through the top floors, but on the male side of the dorms. Fortunately, she was not successful in conjuring up light for more than brief flashes so she had not moved more than a few steps through the door.

"Hey." I spoke gently so as not to scare her.

She sniffed and wiped at her cheek. My brows dropped into a scowl as I realized she was crying. "Are you okay?"

"You need to go, right? Need to get to her?" she asked and moved further down the dark corridor. The dorms began on the floor below. This space held decorations and other memorabilia for events, parties, and other campus functions throughout the year. The attic of the university if there was such a thing. There were several doors that were labeled and I had no doubt that like the messenger bag she was rifling through, those doors may open to entire buildings worth of items rather than the size of a regular room.

"What are you looking for?" I asked a question rather than answering hers.

"A flashlight." She snapped her fingers and then looked into the bag as the little light faded. It was about the brightness of and had the stamina of a cheap matchstick.

"Eleanor." I moved closer and she shook her head. I could see clearly in the dark, so there was no point in her hiding from me. I gulped and then asked, "Was it that bad?"

She stopped searching and the light

completely faded. She looked my direction and said, "Which part? The part where I was finally feeling like I might belong here? The part where I thought for a flash of a heartbeat you might be interested in me beyond tutoring? Or." She snorted a laugh that was far from funny. "Or the part where you clearly scented your mate in that pub so it didn't really matter if we were at the start of something because the only thing I know about..." She stopped talking. Gargoyles. Not demons. Not all gargoyles, just my kind, would flush so their mate would know. "But you said you..."

"I didn't expect—"

Of course, she could not see me, but that didn't keep me from smiling when she put it together. With a gasp of shock she said, "That was you! In the library! You... stabbed me in the ass."

"I did not. You ran into me. I was... thinking." Not a total lie. I was thinking about her ass and then she backed into me resulting in a poke.

Her arm swatted out at the darkness and instead of backing away, I moved in closer, reached for her wrist and when my fingers felt her flesh again, I tugged and hoped she would move forward.

To my relief, she stepped closer to me. At the risk of being too bold, I admitted, "You. I scented you. No one else."

Then, before she could process that, I leaned down as I pulled her in closer and kissed her. So soft. So tender. It took a lot to get me drunk and the two pints I had at the pub had barely started a buzz that my body burned through before I exited the pub doors. I was sober, but feeling… something else. High maybe? Light, strange.

It felt like she was sucking a part of my soul out of me and depositing a part of hers the moment our mouths opened, tongues clashed, and the sweet exploration turned into a heated duel. I could feel myself getting hard, growing desperate for more than the smooth slide of her tongue against mine exploring the nodules that formed along the center. I was made for a woman who could handle a bit more. I was made for a demon or a gargoyle mate. What I had was a witch and her frail human body with absolutely no defense against the rougher elements of mine.

Her breathing was ragged as she

lifted her face up as if to press her lips to mine once more. It was enough to remind me that I wanted, needed more from her, but this was not the time or place to see if she could handle all of me or run screaming that she changed her mind.

I gulped and turned my head, bent a bit more so I could lick along her neck, feel her pulse thundering beneath warm flesh. My hands circled her wrists before she became too handsy. I moved her hands to push under my shirt. She needed little encouragement to push that up and then pull it off of me. My wings popped out as though they had been waiting for that.

Her hands slid along my chest as my lips moved back in and kissed along her neck, that cleavage. Expanding to flight width, the wings wrapped forward, enveloping, shielding us from any sudden visitors. Anyone could pop out of one of those rooms and at any time. Though the darkness would indicate no one else was up here, this place was unpredictable and the staff were just as secretive as the students.

"Braz." The whisper of my name was cut short by a feminine sound I would replay in my mind on repeat later.

Her breasts filled my hand to overflowing and I laved, feasted on her sounds of pleasure. When her hips moved as if they would hump the air between us, I slid my other hand down to cup her ass. It was then I realized her pants had a zipper and button on the back.

"Turn around." The command was

both too deep and demanding for my own ears, but she let go of my shoulders where her hands had found purchase and turned to face the wall.

Her fingers slid along a wing and that did strange things to me. “These are very soft.”

True, they were the softest part of my entire body, I was sure of that.

“You’re…”

“I like them.” She must have realized I wasn’t sure how to say it. After two years of studying tactics at the university level, I was suddenly back in my pre-college days when I was exploring everything with a brand new perspective and unsure how any decision would turn out. Then, it had been typical adventuring, getting into mischief with friends, and testing our metal.

Now, this delicate creature pinning her shirt over her shoulders as I tried to keep a steady hand and undid the button on her pants, could destroy me with a word. A look. A sound.

Careful. I had to be careful with her. She was mine and I had to take care of her. Please her. Make her want me tomorrow as much as she wants me right now. Keep making her want me until it won't matter that we aren't the same genetic species. We're close enough. We had to be for me to have this strong of a reaction to her. Sure, it didn't happen on sight, but only gargoyles of my mother's line had that problem of flushing colors and mating for life. Demons, like my father, had other priorities, like ambition. Eleanor was not my conquest. I knew that for sure. I wouldn't care about all of these little details like the way she was wiggling as I unzipped the zipper if I just wanted to fuck her.

I wouldn't be sliding these pants down and over that lush ass at a painfully slow pace as I lowered to my knees behind her. She couldn't see it. Probably hadn't even looked, but I could. My eyes noticed the two distinct little marks where she had backed into my horns. They lit up at my touch. *Huh.* That was not in anything anyone had told me about before. I leaned closer and licked over the two dots. The way she shivered and called out to me had me mentally putting chains on my demon to keep him at bay. All aspects of my personality wanted her, but yeah, we were going to take this one step at a time.

CHAPTER SEVEN

Eleanor

MY SENSES WERE on overload. I couldn't grasp any one sensation stronger than the other for more than a moment before the lightning running wild and striking out throughout my veins would hit again. I was embarrassed by the amount of me exposed, but it was completely dark except the slightest glow radiating from him like an aura.

I was sure he could see everything, but I couldn't even see my own hands on the cold concrete wall in front of me. My legs could only move so far apart since I still had my shoes on and my pants were around my ankles.

That deep, husky voice ricocheted off the wall as he said, "Lean—"

What the hell was I doing?

I was leaning forward. Scooting into the position he was guiding, steadily losing my mind, and surrendering my body to... whatever Braz actually was. A demon, sure, a gargoyle? Made some sense, but also... his parents had to be from some very unique lines to— "Oh wow. Wow. I. Wow. Okay. Um. Braz. Braz."

That tongue was something to explore with my own human shaped muscle, but his nodules were doing more than sparking lightning as he moved closer to my soaked core. I mean I knew there was not a waterfall there, but my thighs were slick from arousal before he spread my legs. That was what he had been exploring, carefully so as not to stab me in the ass again with one or more of his horns.

I wanted to touch them. Hold them. Move his head exactly where I needed it to be so I could—

"I thought the scent was intoxicating, but your taste is… addictive."

If he wanted a coherent response, he should not have licked that long tongue with those blessed ridges over my clit. I probably said something, but the tongue was still moving and any worries about his makeup and how that would work with mine just... didn't seem to matter. If he felt this good, he couldn't be bad for me.

I held onto the wall and scooted a fraction of an inch further, forced my feet to shift a bit more, giving him any and all access to that spot so he could work all the magic he wanted. The tremors began at my toes, radiated up the backs of my legs, made every muscle and tendon I didn't even realize could work so hard, strain and tense until I shattered in a series of spasms that made my hands slip on the wall. I lost my grip and went face forward only to be caught by the velvety smooth wing that had been providing privacy for this event.

I was an exceptionally smart person in the Earth realm, a basic witch in this one, and if Braz asked me my name right now, he would realize I could only say his. Which I hoped was what I was in fact saying but my ears were still thundering, my body still trembling with aftershocks, and twitches that probably made me look like I needed to go to the infirmary.

The next thing I knew, a large, warm body was settling next to me, behind me as the wing pulled me closer. He whispered as he gently untucked my shirt from my shoulders and where I had it pinned with my arms and said, "I'm sorry."

My brows knitted and I was confused. "Wh..." I gulped and found my backbone because I couldn't chicken out. I needed to ask and know the truth. "Why?"

He whispered, "This wasn't the best place to do that. You could have hit that wall. Anyone could have walked out of those doors or through the one at the end of the hall. I just... couldn't... wait to... kiss you."

My heart was now outpacing the other sensations in my body as I admitted, "Don't be sorry. If I didn't have to focus on the wall I might have been loud."

He snickered and I turned to look at him, even if I couldn't see him, only feel him. "What?"

He touched the tip of my nose and said, "My little witch. You were very loud."

I could feel my jaw drop as I gasped in shock. I guess the blood pumping in my ears had made the sounds a bit dull, plus he had better hearing than the average being, so… how was that fair?

He leaned in and kissed my lips before I could get too offended and say more. “Someone is coming up the stairs. Let’s go.”

I popped up and stumbled, but he steadied me. Shirtless, he guided me as I pulled at my pants and we went out the same door we had entered. The night sky was clear so we could see all of the stars. He was behind me, fastening the button on my pants when we heard the door creaking open. The next thing I knew, we were airborne.

When we landed again, we were near the school, but not so close anyone would have seen that unless they were looking. I turned to look up at my tutor who had just taught me a whole lot in a very little amount of time and asked, "Where is your shirt?"

"Oh shit." He looked and then shook his head. "I forgot to grab it."

"Are you going to get into trouble?" I asked, worried about what this would do to him, me, us.

He shook his head no. "I'll tell them I was looking for weapons in that storage room." He looked beyond us and said, "But maybe you should walk a bit ahead, go in before me. I don't want your reputation to be in question because I'm shirtless and you're... a bit... disheveled."

I gulped and nodded, but that hurt. He didn't want to be seen with me. He attempted to smooth my hair, but I pushed both of my hands into it and tied the back in a knot. I said a quick spell, expecting it to totally fail, but it worked for a change and my hair stayed in place. I was so relaxed and satisfied that I didn't even realize I hadn't asked if he... also experienced the relief of a release until I opened the door to my room and slipped in quietly. My roommate was sleeping like a corpse. The eye mask and product combined with the statuesque pose gave me the creeps, but I was a bit too high on the orgasm endorphins to care much about more than a shower.

Once I crawled into bed, I reached back and rubbed the spot where he had poked me in the ass. He did that. As a gargoyle, he let me back right into him and... *huh*. Where did I read something about... *whatever*. I had other things to focus on. I'd find out soon enough if Braz was going to be more than my defensive arts tutor. If what we did was going to be our little secret. If what we do would be our little secret. I nodded. Yes. I liked that idea better. Keeping this to ourselves. Whatever it would lead to, I could finally have something of my own to look forward to. I wasn't exactly sure how my father would take knowing I was… what? Hooking up? With a unique paranormal being.

I rolled to my side and faced the wall. *What am I doing?* I just met him. He… oh but he made me feel sooooo very good for the first time in my life. I wasn't thinking about anything but chasing that feeling. And if he wanted to give me orgasms of epic proportions this year, well. I was going to let him.

CHAPTER EIGHT

Brazrothan

"YOU OKAY, MAN?" Thirst asked as I settled into the chair in the common area of our room. This would normally house three or four of us, but they had plenty of rooms. They only made us double up just to remind us this was college not our personal playground. Though in many ways this had been exactly that for a group of us. Nothing major, just pranks and rowdy excursions into forbidden places such as the woods.

"Yeah. Sure. Of course. Why?" I should have stopped at one word.

He snickered and said, "Okay then."

In true brothers by other mothers and fathers, for that matter, he got up and went to bed. But not before patting me on my shoulder and saying, "Lucky."

Yeah. I was always known for my luck. How was it lucky?

Let me count the ways:

1. I'm a paranormal species anomaly, so the likelihood of me finding a mate like me… yeah right. Not lucky.

2. I'm Eleanor's tutor. *And her mate. Dammit! Stop that.*

"Stop what?" Thirst asked.

"Nothing. Sorry." I leaned forward

putting my elbows on my knees and my hands on my face. I closed my eyes and mentally said to myself, stop that.

I could have sworn I just laughed at myself, but I might have heard Thirst laughing at me from the adjacent room. The arch did nothing to separate the sleeping from the living space.

I got up, gathered my things, and headed to the showers. I could use an ice cold one about now.

As I walked, I continued my list. Lists made me feel like I had at least some form of plan, control, something.

3. She's a freshman. She has four years here and I have two left. *So two years together and then I could teach or— STOP THAT!*

4. She's a witch and I'm… a fucking mess. That is what I am. A fucking mess.

I gave up on the list and indulged in the absolute coldest shower the water would provide for several minutes before actually cleaning up. I didn't touch the soap until her scent was completely gone from my senses. I opened my mouth, tilting my head back and letting the water fill it several times until I could barely taste her on my tongue. All the nodules slowly receded once she was clear of those giant taste buds and I began to feel more like the monster I knew myself to be.

Precision and planning were two things I prided myself on and what I had done this evening was neither planned or precise. I let the flash of memory at her almost face planting into the wall filter in and shook my head. Smooth, Braz. *Real smoo-ooh shit.* She called me that. Braz. I didn't have a nickname. Everyone just called me Patrick. Braz. I liked it. Liked that she said it. That she didn't see me as a teammate, a buddy, a—

"Fuck's sake. Is the heat out?" Caesar, one of the debate team members had just slapped my ass. He went several down and turned the water on. No doubt as hot as it would go. I typically did that too. My inner demon was not pleased with this shower, but my gargoyle and my hormones were finally settled.

"No, jackass. I just wanted to cool off." I soaped up and moved the dial to warm, not hot for a change.

"You missed it." He was loud, so I knew whatever it was it was something I should have been with my friends to see.

"What?" I asked, indulging him.

"The unicorn." He practically whispered that.

I snorted a laugh and shook my head. If they had seen the unicorn, Thirst would have said that right when I walked in the door.

"You sure about that?" I asked.

"Fuck you and them to. I know what I saw." He flipped me off and went back to showering, mumbling about how no one believed a demon.

He was known for exaggerating. Not lying so much as seeing what he wanted to see. Like he swore he saw Professor Wentworth curse someone. That student did end up in the infirmary, but it was for ingesting too much sugar and having a low tolerance, which everyone of that species knows, and not because the

Practical Application of Curses professor had it out for him.

As I dried off, I realized in my haste to escape the pub, get Eleanor alone or away from me, or whatever my head was warring with during that flight, we did not stop to get her a wand. As a new witch, sometimes having a wand to project intentions through would help the spell focus and cast. It... filters the emotions and focuses more on the intent of the spell. She probably would not have been caught reshelving books if she had a wand. Of course, I wouldn't have caught sight of her bent over and... I shook my head and the thoughts.

"Settle down," I whispered to my inner core which was threatening to heat up and seek her out. "We will see her tomorrow."

But that really wasn't soon enough for me.

CHAPTER NINE

Eleanor

SLEEPING BEAUTY, ALSO known as my roommate, literally woke up to the sounds of birds singing to her. Like, that was her alarm. I felt my right eye open and I looked across the space at her. She sighed and slid to a sitting position at the edge of her bed and for one moment, when she thought no one was looking at her, she frowned.

My mind wondered what made her make that face, but the next moment, the smile was back in place and the noise was the ringing of the crystal ball my father had sent to me. I opened my eyes and popped out of bed saying, "Sorry. He must not realize the time."

We hadn't spoken since the first day, but after last night, I was feeling more relaxed so I just... didn't care about that little hiccup.

"I'm going to prepare for the day." She got up, put her hand on top of the five layer beauty case that was about hip height and on wheels and said, "Come on, Case."

The case wheeled itself behind her as if it were a pet. I went to the closet I had shoved my father's communication device in and removed the velvet cloth I had wrapped it in a few days after that little incident. I placed it on my desk and took a seat. "Hello."

"I wasn't sure if you were going to answer. I've tried a few times, but..." He didn't sound like himself. My father was a man of influence and power. Not unsure and cautious about anything.

"I'm sorry about that. It was..." I gulped. "Why did you tell them I had taken Defense Against the Dark Arts studies? They put me in an advanced class."

He winced and admitted, "How could I not? I... know you can defend yourself. You learn so fast, and... how could I tell them I didn't teach my own child when they use my book to teach the basic courses?"

I could see his dilemma, but it did not change one thing about mine. I sighed and said, "Father, my magic does not work as well here as it does at Grandmother's or even in the human realm. I can do all sorts of spells at home, but I'm… lost here. Things don't work. It's like I'm missing a piece of a puzzle I didn't even know I was supposed to be putting together."

"I'm sorry, Darling. When you were summoned—"

"Summoned? You made me fill out an application." My brow shot up.

He cleared his throat and said, "I wanted you to think it was your choice and you had hoped since finding out you had magic… so, when I got the letter, it just… made sense to create an application so I could be sure this is where you wanted to be."

"Is that why you sent this ball? On my first day? Because you already knew I... was going to struggle?" I frowned and felt betrayal and confusion rushing through me. I wanted to cry. I wanted to scream at him. I... wanted to go... hit something.

"I knew there was a chance that you would not be on par with your peers. Are you learning from your roommate? She is exceptional in the arts." He smiled, proud of himself that some influence he had was the reason I was in this room with her.

I had the choice to either tell him the truth or break that cycle and keep the truth to myself. I decided it was time to rebel a bit more and I told him what he wanted to hear instead. I wasn't sure why I was summoned to this academy, but it didn't matter. I was here now and I wanted to be here more than anywhere else. Except maybe in Braz's arms and he was also at this school. By the end of the conversation where I told him about the other classes, some of which I was really feeling okay in, and then told him to give my love to my mother and siblings after he had filled me in on their mundane activities back home. They missed me. I'm sure my parents really missed me since I did most of the caretaking for those two little monsters when my mother was at work.

Maxine returned in an outfit that fit her to perfection. She was also a curvy girl, but unlike me where there were curves and then more softness, Maxine was curvy and also... tone or fit somehow. She pointed and her case went to the closet and opened to sort through whatever she would need next. I took a chance and said, “That is really amazing.”

She looked over at me and said, “I’m going for a walk. Care to join me?”

I looked down at myself and asked, “Give me five to get dressed?”

She nodded and said to the case, “Inventory, Case. I don’t want to find out my face cream is on the last vile when I’m using it. I need to have it on order. Change my address for the delivery.”

Case was more than amazing. Case was like, the personal assistant everyone dreamed of. Inventory. I headed to the common bathrooms and made quick work of morning business and emerged ready to… go for a walk.

Of course, Maxine was not slow. She power strutted from the moment we hit the pavement outdoors. A few steps in and she said, "You're stubborn."

"Um."

"But also keep your business to yourself. I like that part. Everyone is always trying to get into my business, but in the past two weeks you have been content to ignore me. Completely. Oblivious to anything I have tried to bait you with." She kept walking.

"Wha—"

"And that is why I am going to trust you, Ellie." She looked over at me and smiled. Ellie? My family was quite formal so everyone called me Eleanor and my parents sometimes called me Darling.

"Okay." I really wasn't sure what to say, but my father was right, Maxine was an exceptional witch at her age and I needed help in more than just defensive arts.

"There is a merman on this campus." She said it as though the professor and the guy with the blue tint that I had seen at the pub last night didn't stand out like a neon sign was flashing over their heads with the word merman.

"Yes. Two." I nodded.

"Thurston Cambridge is the older brother of my former… well. We weren't lovers, but he was my first love." She seemed to speed up along with her thoughts. "And Dolin Cambridge was not, I repeat not invited to attend this year."

"Oh." I wasn't sure what this was about.

She stopped suddenly and I stopped

too because she turned to look at me and said, "I must stay away from him."

"Okay." I could feel my eyebrow raise.

"You will help me?" she asked.

"Sure." I wasn't sure what the problem was.

At least, not until I saw the pack of beautiful creatures running toward us in some sort of formation. The tall, blonde haired, blue eyed merman was shirtless, wearing only shorts and running shoes. He was such a sight to see. Only, he wasn't what held my focus and attention. It was Braz, running next to him, his chest began to flush with each step they made closer to us.

Someone yelled, "One more lap and then the field."

Lap, field. Those were real words but as the horned monster looking at me as they ran past us smiled, I could barely understand my name much less those directions.

“Come on. They are going to the field.” I snapped to my senses when a very cold hand landed on my arm and tugged.

About halfway to the field I asked the obvious question, “How is this... staying away from him?”

“I’m not speaking to him. I’m just... curious about their fighting tactics. It’s smart for us to know what they do. Observe them so we can defend ourselves against other monsters like them should we encounter them in our lives beyond the school.” She practically dragged me along since I could not keep up with her.

“But why would they attack us?” I

asked, totally oblivious to the politics of this realm if her expression said anything about it.

"Because outside of this realm, in other realms, species have established domains, territories, and if you travel to those places, you could become prey. They could try to drain you of your magic." She explained as we found a spot in what amounted to bleachers.

"Oh." I had only traveled between two realms, but that made sense. Even in the human world there were people looking to take from someone else because they were a tourist. People were kidnapped, murdered, or stolen from all the time when they vacationed in other towns much less countries. It only made sense that would be similar in the magic world if the human realm had so much in common with this one. "But in this realm—"

"Shhh." She pointed. "Some of them can hear exceptionally well."

At that, one of the monsters on the field turned his head toward us. Everyone then turned to look at us. I gulped. We both remained silent until their attention shifted back to their circle of guys and a moment later they were split into groups of seven and one, the coach based on the shirt, called out some words and then a glittery magical dome appeared over all of us.

"We're in it now." Maxine nodded.

"Great." I had no idea what to say. I was less prepared for what was about to happen.

The teams split up and the landscape began to change. We were still in the bleachers, but somehow above them and the screens in front of us appeared from the floor and hovered at elbow height. We could see the entire field on those screens and the numbers lit up designating the players of both teams.

This was the first game I had seen. I only knew I was rooting for whatever team Braz was on, and I had no idea which one that was until the screen lit up and much like Sunday night football back in New York, the players were being displayed, only instead of stats for touchdowns or passes or whatever, they covered their skill sets, monster features, and then kills. Kills?

"Are they—"

"No, not really. They have the dome, so even if they die, they don't die, but ultimately it is about which team kills the other." She said it like that was no big deal. "Again, the dome ensures it is simulated. A kill strike stuns the opponent, but once it wears off they get up and go to the sidelines because, well, they are out of the game. We watch it on the professional level all the time at home. You've never seen this before?"

"No." I gulped and watched with anticipation and anxiety as Braz and his team split up into what could only be tactical formation and both teams began… hunting each other. "No. I have not seen anything like this before."

It could have been hours or days before the competition ended. I wasn't sure. Braz, Thurston, and two others I had seen that night at the pub were still standing and 10 monsters were in various stages of stunned recovery.

Maxine looked over to me and said, "Exhilarating, is it not?"

I nodded. Sure. Whatever. Between the gasps, the jolts, and the time Braz almost got caught, I was a bundle of nerves and felt more frazzled than exhilarated. A moment later, the dome, screens, and magical environment they had been battling in was all gone. What was left were fourteen sweaty monsters laughing, joking, and slapping each other on the ass, punching each other on the shoulder, or simply high-fiving one another.

They seemed no worse for the wear other than tired. Braz looked up to where we were seated and I smiled. Did a slight finger wave. Thurston elbowed him and they were off to the formation to run out of there.

Maxine said as she stood, “I think he will end up going pro.”

“Who?” I felt like a dumbass around this witch.

“Thurston, of course. Possibly the demons, Remington and Glock. The twins.” She pointed and I realized those were two of the other members of that pub pack. “Now that they have had their training, they will likely end up at the pub. Want to go?”

“I don’t mean to sound like the stupidest witch around, but again, how is this staying away from Thurston?” I asked. Though I also considered it would be interesting to see Braz again. Aside from some facial acknowledgements, he hadn’t spoken to me, so… maybe seeing him at the pub would be a good idea.

“If I know where he is, I can avoid

him." She shrugged. "Obviously."

As a woman ready to stalk her own monster, I had to agree. "Makes total sense."

CHAPTER TEN

Brazrothan

THE SHOWERS WERE loud and filled with chatter that I blocked out. Ellie was at our practice. I hadn't even told her that I had practice. In fact, that was the first time I had played in a while. Coach asked if I could fill in and what I realized was how much I missed it. I missed all of it. The games, the team, and why?

Because I was trying to be above all this college crap?

I was trying to prove that I was the only clear choice for valedictorian when I graduated? I still had senior year ahead of me. I still had this entire year to look forward to and I finally had something to celebrate. A mate. A mate. A mate. I had someone who was there for me even if she didn't know how much that little coincidence had an impact on my performance. I couldn't lose in front of her. No way.

"Patrick!" Thirst shouted though he was right next to me.

"What?" I blinked as I turned to focus on him.

"Damn, man, you got it bad." He looked at my head and said, "Real bad."

I ran my hand up and over my hair

and my… oh shit. My horns. They were… down, like curling, which meant only one thing, I was taken. Off the market officially. Shit. I mean, I knew this might happen, but to present myself as committed when I hadn't even discussed dating with Eleanor. I gulped and then focused until they were standing up again.

Thirst cracked up laughing at me and turned the shower to the sea water valve which he obviously preferred. His light blue coloring grew deeper and scales and other maritime accessories began to appear. Before I could turn my hot as it could get water off, he said, "Did you see who she was with?"

I nodded.

"Is it worth it?" he asked.

My brow went up.

He clarified, "Surrendering."

"So far, yes. But uh... I'm the only one who knows what's happening." He laughed. "Besides you."

"I've wanted that little witch since my brother brought her home." He looked over at me. "I shouldn't."

"You haven't." I reminded him.

"I want to." He rolled a shoulder.

"Are they together?" I knew they were not. Everyone knew Maxine Mayhem's social status. She was a Mayhem after all and they were one of the richest and most notable families in several parts of the realm.

"No," he said as we both turned off the faucets. "Doesn't make it right or any easier."

"No." I imagined it did not. "Well, then. Stay away from her."

"I didn't show up at her practice today." He did some merman equivalent to an animal shake that sent the salt water flying in all directions.

I dried off my face once more with the now damp dowel I was holding and frowned at him. He laughed again. He knew I hated when he did that and he always waited until I had my towel.

"Well." I wrapped the towel around my waist as we made our way to the lockers. "There are plenty of other females around to put your time and attention on."

He nodded. "Right. Tonight."

I wished I had some way to get word to Eleanor to meet me at the pub. I didn't want to put my time and attention into anyone else.

An hour later, I was so excited to see

that Eleanor was already there, I didn't even think twice about heading straight for her... and Maxine. I guess Thirst would have to choose if he wanted to hang with us or the team, but I wasn't leaving Eleanor's side until she pushed me away. "Hey."

She smiled at me and scooted over a bit to let me slide in next to her. "Hi."

Once in the seat Eleanor said, "This is my roommate, Maxine."

I looked up at Thirst still standing at the end of the table as if he couldn't decide if he should sit, go, or—

"You can sit, Thurston. I don't bite." Maxine Mayhem looked like at any moment she may very well eat him alive, but Thirst wouldn't look directly at her. He just slid in silently, stoically even.

This was going to be the beginning of

a really interesting night if those two had anything to do with it.

CHAPTER ELEVEN

Eleanor

Maxine had an interesting approach to staying away from someone. Since Thurston looked as though it was breaking his knees to bend them and sit next to her, I decided she didn't have much to worry about. The guy wasn't into her.

I, on the other hand, was totally into

the guy next to me. I watched with fascination as the pointy horns on top of his gorgeous head extended and then began to... curl back. He looked like he just robbed a ram of their horns by the time it was done. He didn't seem to notice it was happening as he drank his pint, but everyone at the table witnessed it.

"Do they do that when you're... calm?" I asked. Maxine practically choked on her drink. Thurston, who was turned in his seat looking like he could bolt up and out of there at any moment since the moment he sat down, pushed up a little like he was going to leave. Because my left thigh was touching Braz's right one, I knew he just made a sharp movement.

I understood as Thurston frowned at

him and gave him an expression I sure didn't want to be on the receiving end of, Braz may have just kicked him. Thurston settled back into his *ready to bolt* posture.

Braz looked at me and said, "Something like that."

It was a warm, suggestive look and my mind flashed back to that hallway. The velvety wings, the way his tongue brought me to the edge of oblivion and then shoved me over that edge into a mindless bliss that allowed me to... just be for a moment. Without judgment or expectation, I could simply exist and feel pleasure like I had never known before.

I wanted more of that feeling. I wanted more of Braz.

Maxine said, "What do you think?" as she simultaneously kicked me under the table.

"Ouch." I frowned at her. "I think you need less pointy shoes."

She rolled her eyes in a gesture of dismissal and frustration if the breath accompanying it said anything. "No. About getting this food to go and—"

"I'm fine right here." Thurston said and nodded, tapped the table, then grabbed his pint and consumed most of it in two gulps. "Right here."

She was not happy about that, but it wasn't like she was big enough to budge the monster sitting next to her. I looked up at my monster and said, "I'm good either way."

He nodded. "Me too." After an awkward silence that I was only becoming aware was our table's norm, Braz said, "What uh... what did you think of the game today?"

"Exhilarating." I lit up. "One minute I was rooting for you, the next I was wishing I could warn you or do something. There were some close calls."

The blue statue at the end of the table said, "You got that right." He looked at Braz and said, "And this guy. It was like he never left the team."

"You left the team?" I asked.

"Middle of sophomore year I… focused all my time and attention on my studies. I didn't see a future in the sport, so… I… started planning for my future as a professor. Hopefully, maybe, someday… here at the academy." He shrugged.

"Ew." Maxine didn't have food in front of her so we could all assume she was tasting the undesired image of him teaching here. "No. You should start a security company or something. You are way too talented to be wasting away as a teacher."

"I don't think it's a waste." I gulped and put my hand on his arm, defensively. "In fact. I always knew I would be a teacher. I just... never considered it might be someplace like this. You take it for granted because you live in this realm and always have. I... grew up with humans for the most part and... I love it here."

Maxine made the same face and mouthed the same word at me. Then she giggled and I shook my head. Yeah, she was probably the daughter my father always wanted. My whole family probably wanted a diva like that ready to... take over something. Her business mind made me wonder, "What do you plan to do after college?"

Her answer was so immediate it seemed rehearsed. "Take over the family business."

They brought our food and Maxine had another pint with that salad. That's when things got interesting. To no one and everyone, in the middle of a calm and normal conversation about professors and courses, Maxine Mayhem said, "I don't want to run a business. I want… babies."

The blue man next to her choked a bit. He shook his head and got up from the table. "I'll put this on my tab. Nice to actually meet you, Eleanor. Braz." He looked at the beautiful, sad, drunk blonde and said, "Max"

That had her head and lips lifting as

she smiled up at him. Then her face contorted a bit and she said as he walked away, "Am I drunk?"

Braz nodded and looked over at me. "Oh she is pissed all right. Come on. I'll get you both back safely."

I wanted to strangle her for having that second pint. One was enough to make me tipsy. Three was like water to the monsters. Braz had only had two and a half.

Once we were at the school, I felt torn. One part of me wanted to be a friend for the first time in my life and help Maxine up the flights of stairs to our room. Or the bathroom. Either one. The other part of me wanted more time with Braz.

He must have read my dilemma because he leaned over and whispered,

"Open your window when you get in. I'll meet you there."

"Bu—" He winked and I understood immediately. He could fly. I nodded and put my arm around my friend's shoulder as I guided her to our dorm room. I had a friend. A really strange, yet wonderful friend.

"I just want to live by the ocean, have a bunch of babies, and be a mom. I never really had a mom. I had two high powered executives who gave me everything I ever wanted, except their time." A big, fat tear slipped down her cheek. My father may have business expectations for me, but he did spend time with me. My mother had me at her side in the office and always took me to and picked me up from school.

"I'm sorry." I understood now why she

was always looking at the closet where the communication ball was. My parents were messed up, but hers hadn't sent a crystal ball to talk to her, see how her day was going, how the first week of school or the second had gone. "Parents just suck sometimes."

She sniffed and said, "Don't tell anyone I—"

"Never." I shook my head. "You can trust me."

I wasn't sure if I could trust her, but I felt confident she could trust me. I asked, "Do you need Case? The bathroom?"

She shook her head and got into bed. I pulled her shoes off and put them on the floor next to her bed. I covered her with the soft blanket that hung over the foot of her bed and said, "I'll check on you in a bit."

I opened our window and then moved her empty trash bin from under her desk next to her bed, just in case she needed that.

I heard a masculine whisper, "She okay?"

I jolted, but should have expected him since I literally just opened the window for him. I let out the startled breath and smiled at his handsome face. His horns were up one moment and then curling again. I walked to the window and propped my elbow on the ledge and asked, "Why are they doing that?"

He cleared his throat and said, "Do you want to go for a walk?"

I nodded, looked at the door. "I can—"

He reached for me through the window. "Come on out."

I looked down. Huge mistake. "Uhhhhh."

"Trust me. I've already flown you way farther than from your window to the ground." He tugged and my pulse began racing with anticipation, fear, excitement. I pushed up and felt more awkward and clumsy than ever before in my life as I made my way to sit on the window ledge. Once I was facing him, legs dangling, he smiled brightly and said, "You ready?"

Hell no. "Of course I am."

CHAPTER TWELVE

Brazrothan

I MOVED IN and lifted her into my arms, where she belonged. Now. Forever. I liked the sound of the little gasp she made when we began to fly. I wasn't going for a walk in the woods at this hour. I wasn't going to walk this close to campus either. Nor town. It was a weekend and students were everywhere.

Everywhere except one place I knew would be peaceful and quiet.

When my feet landed on the ground on the same part of the roof where we landed that first night, I felt like walking her through that door and reliving that moment all over again. Tasting her, making her tremble with pleasure, making her gush all over my tongue.

"Wow. They are still growing." Her observation almost made me drop her, but I held a moment longer because she asked, "Is it rude to... touch or—"

"You can touch anything you want." I didn't mean that. I could feel the flush of heat and knew the rush of color would be spreading soon. I hadn't mated with my mate and this physical behavior unique to my species or combined species as it were, made things awkward in the physical revelation department.

Her fingertip explored the very tip of one of my horns. "It's not as pointy as it was in the library."

"Neither of them are. Nor am I." I sighed and closed my eyes, leaned into the touch, refusing to set her down now she was actively touching me.

"So are you going to tell me about this?" She ran her finger up the side and around until she touched my hair where she wrapped a lock around her finger and slid it closer to her nose. "It's so soft and smells so good."

I had to tell her. "Well. I uh…" I gently placed her on her feet and reached for the hand that slid free of my hair. She held my hand and it reminded me that while she was curvy and lush in all the right places, the right ways, she was still so much smaller than me. "I know you understand that I am not like any demon or gargoyle you've read about in class or books. I'm a hybrid species and it causes any other dormant genetics from either parentage to... pop up or display itself without warning."

She nodded. "I know."

"So the color change... it's... to let my uh..." I gulped. "Mate know that she has been located. It is a call for her to come to me. It's usually a color the mate is fond of."

That was true, she always had something almost magenta slash pink but not quite on her. The pens she used. The notebook cover. Her bag. I realized just how much I noticed every little detail of her without consciously being aware I was taking all this inventory.

This evening it was the top she was wearing. It made her deep brown eyes almost appear to have red flecks in them.

"So you are turning... this shade of pink for... me?" she asked and seem more intrigued rather than frightened by that.

"Yes." It was like a planet just lifted off my shoulders. The truth was out there. Now, she would either make my life complete and we could begin building a future at whatever pace she set... or, she would destroy me and my heart and I would... I had nowhere else to go. I'd just...

"Thank you." She touched my chest. "I mean, it's... flattering to think that someone like you would even look at someone like me. Are you sure because

I'm... not..."

I stopped walking the short path around the edges of this particular section of the roof. I tugged her around to look at me. I let go of her hand and then placed both of my hands on either side of her face, resting my thumbs on her cheeks and my hands along her delicate neck. The pulse practically punched my fingers her heart was beating so fast. I shook my head and made sure she looked me in the eyes as I said, "You. Are. Everything. To me. This instinct does not make mistakes. I may be an anomaly, but I trust that I would not reveal all my secrets to just anyone. You're special, Eleanor. You're kind and caring. You love it here and so do I. You're smart and resourceful. But most of all, you are mine."

She licked her lips and smiled up at me. “So that means… you’re mine?”

I nodded. “Faithfully.”

The little witch had a glint of mischief in her eye as she said, “And your horns are curling because of me?”

“I doubt I can force them to stand again unless to defend myself, though I double anyone would want to be hit with these either.” I titled my head. “It signals to some types of demons that I am not available.”

“Ah. And how do I signal that I’m not available if you have colors and magical horns and—” I cut her off with a kiss. Not kissing her was making me crazy.

When we broke that kiss, I admitted. “I’m not sure, but I doubt anyone will try to approach you for romantic liaisons with me by your side at every waking moment I'm available to be there."

She giggled and said, "Well then. Let's look at our schedules and plans and make sure we get some alone time."

I pulled her in close for a hug, forgetting about the fact that my groin was also showing mating signs that I never wanted anyone else but her to see, though I was still worried about what she would think, how and if she could handle that... activity.

In a breathy whisper against my lips, she said, "May I?"

I closed my eyes and clenched my jaws. I nodded.

Her hands began to roam over my chest, my shoulders, back to my chest and down my abdominals. I wouldn't stop her. She had to know and sooner rather than later was for the best.

Delicate fingers slid over my pants and the erection bulging beneath them. She had one word for my ego. “Wow.”

CHAPTER THIRTEEN

Eleanor

I GULPED AND tried not to let my fingers tremble as his eyes closed and his head went back on a deep moan. My name a whisper on his lips, I could barely hear it over the sound of my heartbeat thumping in my ears.

This was not a person size penis. At least, no person I had ever seen and since I went to school in the human realm where cell phones filmed or photographed everything, I had been shown more than a few over the years. The same nodules that expanded on his tongue as he kissed me also seemed to be... developing on his penis. I was so tempted to undo the pants and expose him to my sight. When I touched the top button on his pants, the door to the roof opened.

I didn't have the chance to say anything before we were off the roof, in the air, and flying. I opened my eyes and tried to enjoy it this time, but as he swooped one way and the next, I found myself getting a bit dizzy. I was never very good at video games and this reminded me of one of those live action ones except I had no control over the destination, how fast or slow we were going, or… where.

The wooded areas surrounding the campus were filled with unpredictable results. Cautionary tales abound and I had only been here a couple of weeks.

I supposed it was a testament to his predicament when he landed us and immediately pulled me in for a kiss as his body pressed against mine and my back pressed against… velvety wings instead of a tree trunk. I teased the nodules on his tongue and let my instincts guide me as I moved my hand down and between us.

The sounds he made as I touched him were intoxicating. Did he enjoy my reactions as much as I was enjoying his? Impossible. This was the most magical thing I had ever done in my life. I unsnapped the top button and then the next and the next. There were no underwear beneath the fabric, just him.

My fingers slid along the bumpy length. When I was at the base, I realized my hand was not large enough for my thumb to touch my fingers. I kept the grip and stroked upward, slowly, feeling every hard bump along the top and bottom expand to greet my touch and then settle as I moved upward. I wanted a better look at this part of him. "Set me down."

He shook his head. "Don't stop. Please."

I bit my lower lip and then leaned in closer to his neck as I gave a hard squeeze and said, "I'm not going to stop."

In increments so slow I wondered if he would have just dropped me if he were less focused, he eased me to my feet. I moved to my knees and said, “You’ll have to adjust.”

Didn’t take more than the statement for him to readjust his stance for me to be face to penis level. His fingers planted against the tree, the wings still providing coverage so no passerby could see critical viewing areas.

I took my time, explored at leisure the visual delight that both intrigued and frightened me. When he began having what could only be viewed as uncontrolled twitches in his knee or hips, I said, “I’m a virgin.”

“So am I.” He dug what I now understood were claws that had emerged from his fingernails into that tree’s bark.

I was stunned by the response, but understood that some creatures mate for life and… while I was brought up too human to believe that was true for everyone, I hoped that it would be true for us, especially if my body wasn't capable of letting him into it.

I'd try my mouth. If I could put it in my mouth, surely, I could make it fit in my vagina another time.

I let my tongue explore the tip and the taste of him. I opened wide and slid the tip into my mouth, barely past my lips when his hips jerked him forward and further into my mouth. The upper and lower ridges slid against the roof of my mouth and the top of my tongue.

My jaws were straining as the slight slide back and buck forward seemed like something he couldn't even control. Sounded like something he couldn't even control. I felt a few slivers of wood pelt the top of my head and slide down the back of my hair. He was going to destroy that tree before this was over if it didn't end soon.

I put both hands together, around him, and stroked. He cried out, sounding like a wild creature calling out to the night for salvation. Two strokes later and he was spilling into my throat. The way his entire body went rigid made me wonder if he, like me, would lose balance. He did not. Fortunately, as I doubted I could catch him.

An endless flow of liquid streamed from him as the orgasm kept going the longer I stroked. Until his hand came down to cover mine and halt me. I pulled back, gulping what I could. Aware there was more dripping down my chin, sliding down my neck.

His eyes were glowing when I looked up at him. He blinked down at me and then reached with his clawed hand as the nails became more… typical looking and touched my chin. Wiped at the fluid still dripping. I licked out and touched my tongue to his thumb. He shifted it up for me to suck the remaining semen from it. I closed my eyes and made a humm sound before saying as he pulled his finger from my mouth, "So good."

"I'm going to keep you forever." He meant it. Glowing eyes and fully curled horns, this monster was mine.

I stood up feeling like I was worth every bit of my father's fortune. I moved in closer to him and realized there were new sounds around us. He did too. He fastened his pants quickly, pulled me in closer and then pushed off the ground.

I didn't look back. I didn't look down. I curled against his chest and felt the warmth of it radiating around me. The flight back must not have been nearly as volatile as the flight into the woods since I woke up to the sound of my roommate making use of that trash can.

I popped up and out of my bed touching my neck only to find that portion of our mess had been cleaned up.

I rushed to Maxine's side to pull her hair back, a task Case could not do though the piece of luggage seemed concerned about her nonetheless as it kept opening its various compartments and offering her different things. None of which would help. "It's okay, Case. I'll help her."

All the drawers shut, but Case did

not go far.

CHAPTER FOURTEEN

A month later…

Brazrothan

SHE WAS FEISTY today. Three weeks into wielding that wand she had named Wanda the Working Witch's Wand and her confidence had exploded. I'd like to think that had something to do with me and my tutoring too, but honestly, she took to defensive arts like Thirst took to salt water. Naturally.

I felt the zap and reached back to rub my ass. I turned and she twirled Wanda and said, "Gotcha."

"I'm going to get you all right." I chuckled, but I was really impressed she snuck up on me like that.

She did this little wiggle I wasn't even sure if she was aware of, and then turned and started running. I loved chasing her. The parts of me that needed to claim and conquer were growing more anxious every day to strip her naked and bury deep into her core.

We had taken to sneaking around and finding pleasure in hands, mouths, tongues. It was enough and not nearly enough every time. When we weren't fooling around, we were playing around. Chasing each other or... we were doing this. As she came to a tree not located in the vast forest and settled down patting the spot next to her, I smiled. It was my turn to lay back with my head on her lap as she played with my horns and my hair.

We talked a lot, and about everything. Sometimes it seemed strange to think I had only known her a month when it felt in my bones like I had known her my whole life. As though my life had not really begun until she was in it. I crossed my hands over my abdomen and reminded her, "I have a game this weekend."

"I know." She cleared her throat. "I uh. I noticed that there are no… witches or… females on the team."

My eyes flashed open and the first word that popped out of my mouth was,

"No."

She snickered and said, "Funny. That sounded like you just said no, and you haven't even heard what I was about to say after that."

I wanted to say anything but what fell out next. "No."

"Is that right?" she asked and moved so I had to sit up and look at her.

"Yes." I closed my eyes. Both my demon and gargoyle had control of my mouth and they were outvoting my logical and rational discussion that would explain to her why there were no women, why there were not witches or warlocks for that matter, but all my primal brain parts could understand was how dangerous it was for us... monsters. No fucking way was my mate going out there. No. Hell no. No.

"You don't even want to hear what I have to say?" she asked.

I tried not to say no again, but that only meant my head shook no as the answer.

"Well then." She got up and looked down at me and said, "Your loss."

My what? I didn't understand what that meant. I did understand that the honeymoon was over because instead of snuggling and teasing each other to the point we would sneak off and give one another mutual pleasure, I was watching her lush ass as she walked away.

"Shit." I practically huffed out my next breath.

About that time, Thirst walked up and said, "Guess you got the news."

"News?" I asked.

"Yeah. Some of the magic wielders

want to play the game so... the school is going to allow them to try out." Thirst shook his head. "Probably won't be a long session."

A few wizards walked by and gave us a head bob of acknowledgement. One said, "Finally giving us a chance to be on the team."

I looked at Thirst as he looked down at me. I said, "I don't think they understand how the dome works."

"Nope." He shook his head. "And I don't know what magical spell is going to both be a spell that ensures none of us die, just get stunned, and that no other magic is used in the dome so they or the fans can't cheat is... someone is going to get hurt."

"Not Eleanor." I got up and looked the direction she had walked, but she was no longer in view.

He sucked in a breath and said, "Maybe if they kill Maxine, I can stop being an awful older brother."

"Not to mention a total dick to Maxine." I couldn't even imagine that being an option to avoid a mate. He could say whatever he wanted, act however he wanted, which to her was just shy of being cruel since he ignored her, ran from her, and literally one time hid from her after she saw him.

"Her family didn't like my brother who is the best of my family. What the hell makes me think they will suddenly be all mer-folk friendly if she hooks up with me? What makes you think my brother won't try to kill me?" He asked as we headed toward the field instead of toward the building.

"He didn't get invited." I reminded him.

"Not everyone gets invited when they would typically go off to college. This isn't a linear program for everyone. It's not like the human realm." Thirst reminded me.

I couldn't say anything that would make his situation easier. I put my hand on his shoulder and gave a squeeze then let go. We were heading toward a nightmare. My little witch was not about to endure the trials, even if they downscaled them for magical people rather than monsters. We knew what we were. Our ancestors knew and we lived here, in this realm, in relative peace and acceptance. The human realm experienced more divisiveness than this one. Class was an issue no matter what realm one lived in. Still, here, until now, we protected those who were more human than not.

I saw my mate talking to Maxine and a few other females, both monster and magical. I didn't understand why they wanted to be in this game with us. Why, if they wanted to play so badly, they didn't make their own game. Why take this from us?

CHAPTER FIFTEEN

Eleanor

I WAS FIRED up. I didn't think things would always be perfect with Braz, but until this afternoon I hadn't thought I would be so… mad or frustrated. I didn't actually want to play this game, or be a part of it. I wanted to know what he thought, how he saw this opportunity he clearly knew nothing about. Maybe our time together was causing him to be too distracted from other things like notifications about trials.

Maxine was the one who wanted to try out for this. Her last name was starting to fit her more every day like one of those custom made outfits in her closet. Mayhem. Yeah, she was living up to that more and more as her… well, stalking efforts were starting to worry me.

This was a testosterone victory though, but the wizards and warlocks knew they couldn't just go after a change in the game without including the females so the lady monsters and the rest of us were also invited. This was the trial. We would have to pass a series of tests to determine if we would or could survive the training.

The announcer came on and the field fell to silence as the voice said, "This is simply to see if those of you who want to play this game are actually equipped to do so. There are things you may not realize. Sacrifices you will have to make to play by the rules. Those rules ensure the warriors who display great abilities for our entertainment don't die in the process of earning your cheers."

Oof, no one seemed really happy about this, but I supposed it was much like in the human realm where people of a certain age only learn what my mother told me after giving me a ghost pepper at the age of twelve, you may get what you want, but you might not want what you get. I made sure if she did not recommend something from that point on to ask why rather than throw a temper tantrum and summon it from the garden.

"What the hell is that?" Maxine whispered and I opened my eyes. In my hand was a ghost pepper.

I gulped and held onto it. "A good luck charm."

Of sorts. It was a reminder that I was on this field with her because I was throwing a different kind of tantrum. Was I really about to put myself through this just to spite Braz?

"Three laps. Begin." The announcer either made that sound through magic or just fired a weapon. Either way, the crowd began running around the field on a track that, from where I stood, didn't end.

Maxine grabbed my arm and said, "You coming or what?"

I looked at the pepper and said, "I'm not."

"Suit yourself." She took off behind the rest of the pack and while she was by no means a slouch in the physically fit department, she wasn't much smaller than me, so I wasn't sure how much endurance she actually had.

I moved to the bleachers, away from the players who had gathered to watch this preliminary screening. Including Braz. The screen popped up in front of me and I looked up, only then realizing we were all inside this dome and would be until this trial was over. The female monsters were in the lead by far. One exceptionally far ahead of the others.

Then a scattering of male and females endowed with magical powers. I held the ghost pepper and began to feel the tingle of burning sensation. I knew it was exceptionally hot. Most humans would only touch them when they had on gloves. Some wore protective eyewear as being near the things could cause irritation and touching could be enough to send someone to the hospital. This was the longest I had ever held one. Eating one had not severely harmed me, but the burn in my belly and accompanying indigestion was the first time anything like that had happened. I ate jalapenos and other spicy peppers on pizza and nachos all the time.

I sighed. I would really rather be holding a box of nachos right now. The kind we got at the movie theater back home. My mother and I would share... *oh no. How?*

I seemed to be doing magic in a place

I was not supposed to be able to do magic in. As the group began to take a second lap and more than one person was being transported on the safety vehicles that were staged apparently along the course for this very reason, I tried to hide the fact that I had nachos. Best way to get rid of the evidence? Eat it.

Maxine was walking, hands over her head, as she rounded the corner, but she kept going. I had to give it to her. She was sticking to her convictions. I looked over at Braz and his crew and noticed my monster was doing his best to ignore me. Maxine's monster was not being successful at ignoring her. Thurston couldn't sit any closer to the edge of his seat without falling out of it.

By the end of the laps, Maxine looked

ready to collapse. The hydration station was available and she went straight to it. Her face let me know it was not the preferred fancy water she liked to drink with fruit slices in it. I had become a bit of a hydration snob after too many rounds of fruit infused water, so I totally understood.

Of course, the next thing I had in my hand was the water bottle I had left on my desk. Inside of it, the fancy water. I took a sip and then hid the bottle next to me. I was going to get into trouble. No two ways about it, but what could I do? I couldn't compete on that field. I didn't want to fight anyone. I only liked to play fight with Braz. I also couldn't leave this dome until it was lifted. I knew that and many more things my classmates had been unaware of because they were dropping like flies and realizing their wands, their spells, even their curses were not saving them. And this was just the run.

CHAPTER SIXTEEN

Brazrothan

HOW THE HELL did she do that? I looked at my little witch one set of bleachers over eating nachos and then drinking from a container she did not have in her hands before. *How?*

The dome was up, I could see no obvious cracks or issues with it. The coach certainly didn't seem to think there was a problem as he began the next round of exercises. I got up and made my way over to my angry mate and took a seat next to her.

"Why uh. Why aren't you on the field?" My gut twisted though I had been so relieved when she took a seat in the bleachers.

"Oh, now you want to talk about it." She was still pissed at me and I understood why.

"I'm sorry. I knew that saying no was not the right thing to say." She looked at me and I continued, "But it was how I felt and my feelings seem to... override logic where you are concerned. I would never want to see you get hurt and as you can see from just the run, they were not prepared for the mile beyond vision."

"The what?" she asked and I looked

at the screen and slid it over to show her the obstacles that were preventing most of them from getting to lap two or three.

"It changes. Sometimes the ground reaches up to get you. Like that poor guy. Sometimes it slips right out from under you knocking you on your ass, like that one." I showed her a female who was crawling away from what looked like nothing more than pavement. "It's unpredictable."

"Wow." She looked onto the field. "They aren't all back yet."

"Coach will not wait on them either. Everything runs on schedule and discipline and ability is key to being able to meet that schedule." I winked at her and she thought back to a few times I had to sneak to her window for a late night kiss rather than a full evening of playing or studying or both.

"What's up next?" she asked.

"Ah. The fear factor." I pointed at the woodline forming on the field. A handful of people turned and headed to the bleachers, giving up before even attempting it. "It's a version of the forest that surrounds this place. Probably different for every student based on the tales they have heard."

"Is Maxine going to be okay in there?" she asked and I just realized that may have been her concern about this all along.

"I don't know." I had to be honest here. "I just... couldn't let you go in there. Alone."

She looked at the field and the two people running out of there, screaming.

"She's still down there." Eleanor

stood.

I put my hand on her arm. “And you have to let her be there or come here… on her own. Because if you go in there… it will spit you out… beyond the field and into the very forest it mimics.”

“Ooooh.” She lifted her head in acknowledgement. “So if you violate the personal trials—”

“You get thrown into a real trial. Yes. It’s only happened once, but neither of those players have been heard from again.” I looked at the field, at Maxine moving closer to her chance to enter the forest. Then I looked across the bleachers at Thirst. He pushed all the way back in his seat as though he wished someone would just strap him into it. Prevent him from doing what I would have done. I would have gone in there after Eleanor and nothing would have stopped me.

I would have risked both of our lives simply because I would not want her to encounter her greatest fear alone in that forest. It would have been an illogical and irrational reaction because nothing in the dome would actually kill anyone, but it would break a bone or leave a mark now and then. Depended on how fragile the player was. So far, the female monsters were the only ones walking out of there rather than running like their asses were on fire.

Maybe the teams would become co-ed after all. Or maybe they would start their own league. All I knew is that the more the magical humanoids learned about this game from experience, the more they were moving to the sidelines.

"It said there was a test of courage, that's it, isn't it?" she asked. I nodded.

"She's about to go in." Eleanor then focused on Maxine Mayhem and I could have sworn the privileged princess had a light blue aura she did not have before as she moved closer to those trees.

"What did you do?" I asked, but had a more pressing matter to tend to when Thurst stood up. He was a barely leashed creature and starting to look more creaturish than not the more he paced the two seats worth of space between us. The screen only showed her location, not what she was dealing with.

Thirst shook his head, spoke to himself aloud, and when he turned to look at the treeline, myself and several of our team brothers, including the demon twins, launched to hold him back. I wasn't sure if we would be successful. I didn't think anything or anyone would have been able to stop me from going in there after Eleanor, but she was my mate. Solidified. Well, all but one element of that had been solidified.

Eleanor may have been able to use her magic in the dome somehow, but seven monsters against a worried mate was not an even fight. He was winning. As my head cracked against a seat, everything began to spin and blur. "Just give a… min… o… be… kay."

CHAPTER SEVENTEEN

Eleanor

I WASN'T EVEN sure how it all happened. One minute the team of monsters was trying to hold Thurston down and the next...

"I don't know." I meant it. I had no idea how I turned them into toddlers. I just... did.

Professor Edwin Dunlop, Dean of

Students was in his mid sixties, had salt and pepper hair, watery blue eyes, and an eyebrow reaching for his hairline as he studied me for any evidence that I was not telling the truth.

"Professor, I swear, I have no idea how I did that. I just... needed them to be... less intimidating at that moment. To stop before someone got really hurt." I considered when they all turned into little monsters, that was not exactly the result. They were not nearly as physically intimidating, but as they were fighting their too big clothing and popping out of garments naked... yeah, I can see how this would be construed as an act of terrorism or something of that nature. Especially, since so many of us magical mere mortals were sidelined and proven insufficient for the games so quickly.

He steepled his fingers and looked across the large desk he was perched behind on an equally large chair. "Well, fortunately it wore off, but unfortunately, that only made it worse."

I suppose that depended upon perspective. I was sure the female and bisexual population were not too pressed about seeing those monsters in various states of undress. In fact, someone had since mentioned they should consider doing a calendar as a fundraiser for next year's equipment. Like they had anything other than themselves in that arena. I did not like the idea of Braz on someone's wall for them to look at.

"Miss Easternwind, get ahold of yourself." Professor Dunlop slapped the top of his desk and I realized I was letting my thoughts drift a bit too much. I had conjured up some some scissors.

"Sorry, Sir." I placed them in the cup on his desk and said, "These are a gift for you."

He seemed unconvinced as he said, "Yes. I'm sure that was the intent. You... have an unprecedented amount of power flowing through you. I think you may need to study in your room for a week or two, let some of this... wear off before you refuel."

"Refuel? I can't eat for a week or two?" Now I was scared. Yesterday I was worried about being expelled. Today I was worried about losing my cafeteria and travel privileges.

He tilted his head. "Have they not taught you anything?"

"Who? Yes. I mean, who?" I didn't

want to say the wrong thing, but I obviously didn't know who *they* were.

His chair creaked as he leaned back and said, "Oh, so they thought it skipped a generation."

"Sir?"

"Your parents, of course. Your father, the wizard and heir to the Easternwind family trade and business. Your mother, the succubus he met and brought back to school with him when he was in what the human realm considered graduate school. Convinced he had found a way to perfect the defensive strategies for her species, she was both his graduate thesis and the love of his life." He said all that like it should not shock me to my very core, but it did. All the times my father was tired came rolling back to me. "It was a secret then, but—"

"My mother is human. Plain, old fashioned human being." I stood up and shook my head no.

"You take a couple weeks in your room, without Maxine or Patrick. See how you feel about your... academic abilities without them to draw from. The dome... even the school, everything around you is prey if you choose to see it that way. You are the first real enemy of our student body who identify as monsters. You are the first real enemy of the school."

"Then why am I here?"

"The headmistress was curious. I believe she was right." He nodded. "You inherited a great deal of Easternwind magic, but you are capable of amplifying that magic to unprecedented levels because of your mother's talent which only activated when it could no longer resist the urge to feed." He scribbled something on magical paper and then said, "We'll meet again in two weeks. See where we are at with the situation."

"The situation?"

"You. You are the situation. You will either be able to use this power for the good of the realm, of the academy, of your family and friends, or… you will have to be expelled to the realm from whence she originated as if you are a danger to us, surely, you would be the monster should you return to them." He smiled at me and said, "I suggest meditation. Chapter three."

I gulped and left the office. I was stunned, shocked, and now that he said it, and things began to filter through my mind, make more sense, I… could see it.

The faint splash of color reaching out and essentially sipping from magical things.

Here, all this time I was worried about dating a monster, how my parents would react to that. And all along, it was me. I'm the monster, it's me!

I ran up the flights of stairs to my dorm room and slammed the door behind me. I flopped down face first onto my bed and cried for what had to be an hour before Maxine arrived.

"Hey. You okay?" she asked as she sat on the bed next to me and pushed at my hair.

"No. I'm a monster." I pushed up and then away from her. "Stay back. I'm... probably stealing all your powers as we speak."

She snorted a laugh and said, "I don't

think so."

"It's true." I could hardly believe it, but she didn't at all.

"Well, then. Take them. Fat lot of good they did me anyway. I went into the forest and you know what I found? Myself." She groaned and moved to her bed.

"Aren't you supposed to move to anther room?" I asked.

"I told you already, I'm not leaving you here alone to deal with whatever crap they have you thinking. If you were bad for us, you would have turned them into worse creatures instead of babies. I mean, come on. It's not a stretch to think of a group of men roughhousing as a bunch of babies." She seemed to think that was an obvious call. "If they had just stayed by their clothing or held onto their pants like some of them did." She rolled her eyes. "Then when they popped back into adulthood they wouldn't have mooned half the school."

"I feel really bad about it." I did. Mostly.

"After that ridiculous conversation with myself, walking out to that sight was… the best thing that happened to me all day. I mean, I was worried at first. Especially when people kept running out of there, screaming and being so dramatic and all. Then, I got this sense of calm. This sense of… courage that reminded me that I am Maxine mutherfucking Mayhem. Anything in there had better be more worried about me than me about it."

She was removing her shoes as she said that so Case, being the loyal luggage that it was, made clapping noises with its drawers. She smiled at it and said, “Exactly.”

I made a conscious effort to look for my streams, see if I was taking from them. Even Case. But I didn’t see anything. I began to relax, settle, and listen to Maxine jabber on about the rumors and gossip and how the administration was trying to spin the whole thing as some sort of glitch in the dome or something.

The dome had been working since they allowed the sport to be played. Currently, the sport was on pause pending further review. I may have cost some of those guys their future in professional… entertaining? I still didn’t like the idea of them hunting each other for sport, even if it was just a sport here in this realm.

A tap at the window and I was even more concerned. I… turned him into a two year old. An adorable two year old who just got his bell rung by one of his buddies two seconds before becoming a two year old, but that was the straw that broke this… succubi's back. Was that the right way to say it? Refer to myself?

Maxine snorted a sound and got out of the bed and said, "Come on Case. You're too young to be a part of this groveling session for sure."

"What? Am I supposed to grovel?" I looked at the window and the man on the other side of it wide eyed and wondering why I had not gotten up to open it if I was reading his expression correctly.

She laughed as she went to the

window and said, "I'm heading to the showers and then to the cafeteria for a bit. They are supposed to be serving up something extra special for dessert."

She winked at me and said, "Take this out of the door if it's clear."

I got up and followed her and said, "What are you doing?"

"Giving you two some privacy. I'll bring back dessert. For you. He can find his own." She wiggled her fingers in farewell and then slid the scarf so that it stuck out on both sides of the door.

Behind me, Braz said, "She's got a thing for being subtle, don't you think?"

I finally turned to face him and said, "I'm so so sorry."

"For what? Turning us into toddlers? I'm only sorry I don't really remember it all that much. I had three demons standing on various parts of my body since I had the best hold on Thirst." He tilted his head and said, "I know they are saying you are a monster's enemy."

"I'm—"

"You're mine." He opened his arms and I ran into them, hugging him tightly and feeling safe and free to be myself at the same time. "You'll always be mine."

He dropped a kiss to the top of my head. "I want to be yours. Now. Let's bind."

"Are you sure? You don't want to—"

"No. I don't want to wait anymore. If they expel me, this may be the only chance we have to be together the way we both need us to be together." I pulled at his neck and he leaned down for the meeting of our lips.

CHAPTER EIGHTEEN

Brazrothan

THE MOMENT HER lips touched mine, I just didn't care if she could kill me. It was actually a strange relief to know that should we ever encounter someone against our union that she could hold her own. Hell, she could probably defend us both. As a monster of my making I never expected to be vulnerable in so many ways with one woman.

All of my nodules were presenting themselves to her advantage. All of them. The ones now raising on my chest were new even to me. I kissed her for a long time, just enjoying the slide of her wet tongue along mine. I reveled in the slight sounds she made in the back of her throat as my hands shifted to slip her shirt over her head.

Once I had her naked, there was nothing more to do than worship her like a goddess divine. She was flushed, her aura glowing, and so damn pliable after that orgasm I was tempted to push right in, but I would never hurt her and aside from the tip of my tongue or finger, we had neither the space or time to fully prepare her body for this.

I had this moment, right now, and I

was not going to waste it. I slid between her thighs, shifting them wider and focused all my efforts on her clit until she was bucking and mewling again. I pushed a finger into her heat and she didn't stop moving her hips, seeking more. A second stretched her. The third was pushed in at the brink of an orgasm that seemed to drain her of all energy she had left.

That seemed like the right time to me. I moved up her body, kissing, licking, until the tip of my dick slid against the wet, soft warmth of her opening. I kissed her lips as my hips shifted slightly, pushing the head against her and feeling the resistance so keen it almost took out my knees.

Instead of me comforting her in this moment, she reached up and touched one of my horns and said, "Breathe Braz."

I let out the breath I had been holding and shifted a bit to breach that entry. I knew I was lit up like a supernova of magenta and pink everywhere because I was matching her aura.

Slowly, with a lot of patience and persistence, I worked my way into her. Once I was there, she shocked me by saying, "Let's change positions."

CHAPTER NINETEEN

Eleanor

BRAZ WAS TORTURING me. Moving so sweet and slow when he had all those pleasure nodules hitting and then missing and then hitting again. I was going to accidentally cast a spell on him if I wasn't careful, so the shift in position would help me stay focused.

I lifted up and lowered down a few

times, nice and slow but rolled my hips to the perfect angle each time so those nodules hit all the right spots on every lift and lower. I bit my lower lip to keep from keening out a sound of deep pleasure.

In this moment, I was not worried about taking anything from him. I was giving us both pleasure and each increase in speed, every rotation of my hips, each lift and lower deeper, harder, had us both focused on one very common goal, climax.

His hands roamed my naked body with loving purpose and one tug of my nipples was all it took to send me into a vortex of bliss. I knew I had covered my mouth with my hand, bit down on my own flesh to prevent the sound from being too loud in the dorm room. His hands moved to my hips and a more aggressive lift of his hips had me refocused on a new climb. I nodded. Met him with equal vigor and put one hand on my mouth and one on his as we both launched into the next hemisphere with the teeth rattling orgasm sweeping through us.

I was spent. If Professor Caldwell had wanted me depleted of energy, well, this was the way to do it. I didn't even roll off of Braz. I simply fell forward on his large, muscular chest and settled in as though he were my favorite mattress.

"I'm your favorite mattress?" he asked with a chuckle.

"Did I say that out loud?" I barely had the energy to be embarrassed about it.

"Yeah. You did." He stroked my back and then played with my hair as we settled from the experience. "And... this... didn't go badly."

I snickered and said, "No. I think it went rather well. In fact, I think we should do this more often. Maybe that will keep my monster satisfied."

"I don't mind being satisfied this way." He kissed my forehead.

"Let me rephrase that." I lifted a bit and looked at his beautiful face and said, "Your monster. This will keep your monster satisfied."

"I do want to keep my monster happy." He ran a finger along my cheek and said, "And for the safety of myself and everyone around us I will make it my personal mission to ensure you are satisfied as often as you need to be."

I laughed and snuggled up to him again. "I love you. You know that, right?"

He squeezed me tighter and said, "I hoped. I've... loved you since you backed your ass into my horns in that library."

I laughed again. "You liked it."

He laughed with me that time and as I drifted in and out of sleep, I considered my future with Braz. Everything I knew about him, about me, about our goals for the future. Maxine was right. I might be a monster, but I was not going to be the bad monster. I was going to be the hero in this story, I just needed to convince the dean.

***

Two weeks went by and I actually enjoyed the time in my room. I hung out with Maxine and Braz. I studied. I practiced the meditation from chapter three. I did a little workout and I summoned the book from my father's bookshelf that I now understood was his dissertation. No doubt this is why the crystal ball in my closet was chirping for attention. I pulled it out and placed it on my desk. "Hello, Father."

"Hello, Darling. I wasn't sure I'd catch you in your dorm. We... haven't heard from you for a few weeks so... I thought we should check in."

"Did Professor Dunlap contact you about what happened?" I asked and waited a beat for him to respond since he was obviously thinking about what to say to me.

"No, but... I have friends who also have children there and..."

"And they don't believe your theory anymore, do they?" I asked. Was this about me or the book I had in my hand and the fact that he had not tamed the succubus he was now married to and had three children with. She had tamed him. She had hoped that I only had magic in my blood. She was feeding off of his magic and mine and my aunts every time we did something in the human realm. "How is Mother?"

"Worried." He at least had the decency to admit that. "This realm is basic, simple, not a lot of magic here so she can remain calm, feed just enough to sustain herself, primarily off the magic I provide and that garden you made for her."

"Why won't she talk to me like this, on the crystal ball?" I asked.

"Because she may get the... magic lust that she has been fighting for many years. Much like a warrior can get blood lust and lose themselves to the battle, the fight, the killing, she... may absorb magic, Darling, but magic can also fill a succubus to the point of breaking."

That explained why I was using magic in the dome. I had to do something with all of it and didn't know I was consuming so conjuring things helped me process. "So why did you let them bring me here? I could do magic fine in the human realm, basic witch stuff. I get here and I can't even find a book on a shelf without reorganizing half the stacks. Then... it just started clicking and things started to get easy for me." I shook my head. "I should have known something was wrong with me then."

"No. No, Darling. Nothing is wrong with you. You... are exceptional. You always have been, but it wasn't until your magic developed that others could see it, but they didn't believe how special you were. I thought it was just the generational thing. Some of the Easternwinds get stronger powers than others. Knowing your mother was not really just a human led me to think that undercurrent of her species boosted your powers when you got adjusted. Apparently, you just had to... relearn what to feed on. But you found out. You figured it out before anything bad happened."

"I turned an entire team of hunters into children." I blinked at him.

"All men are children, you projected their actions onto them. You didn't murder them, slaughter them. You didn't even make them remain that way until they grew up again. You could have done a lot worse than startle them with childhood for a few minutes." He was animated and serious. I guess Maxine was right since my father didn't seem to think there was a problem. "I know your mother scared them. The realm. She was… in the woods, I couldn't keep her in the dorm and she liked to hunt there so… one day… it was a miscommunication."

My mother was the monster in the great forest. She was the one who ensured those two hopefuls did not return to play the game. I frowned. "She—"

"She did what they did, react to a threat. Only, nothing about their being was enough to withstand her pull and when she got a taste of one monster…

she... couldn't stop. Couldn't. So we came to Earth where there are no monsters like that."

"But there are monsters." I thought back and then my eyes went wider.

"We live in a very safe neighborhood. All the children are safe. She doesn't go beyond our town and our town is right outside of the city where there is no shortage of criminals to sustain her without alerting the authorities." He justified every bit of what I already knew to be true just from the way I remembered her watching the news.

"Would she be able to... eat them all?" I asked.

"I don't know, but we will never find out. Understand? Part of being here is the fact that she can sustain. She cannot return to her realm because she left with me, saved me, a prisoner who went to a place he had no right to be in and came back acting as though it all went to plan. They think I brought her with me as part of my experiment. She brought me back to them because she fell in love with me. She was supposed to kill me. Study me and then put an end to my life." He was being honest and candid in a way that touched my heart because what he was also letting me know is that I was probably never going to be able to come home again.

"Father, am I... a danger to her?" I asked.

"She would be a danger to you, Darling. Now that you have absorbed so much magic that your aura is glowing so bright and pink, I... will be able to see you when I visit your grandmother. I'll bring your brother and sister. I'm sure there is a place for you at the headquarters for the family business. I expanded us to this realm, but we are all family."

He was painting his own idealistic picture of a life I would not be living.

"Then give my love to her, will you? Tell her I am okay and I have control of it. I will be just fine here in this realm, with my mate."

"Did you say your mate?" he asked, startled so he choked on the coffee he was trying to drink when I said it.

"Yes. I've been mated. We both aspire to be professors one day. Right here, at Blackthorn Academy where I will teach the defensive arts and he will teach the offensive ones. We are a perfect match." I nodded.

"Well. It... uh... seems you have it all figured out then. I... knew you were going to grow up fast when you got there, but I did not anticipate... so much." He nodded, seemed caught between happy and sad. "I will do better about determining if your sister or brother have any extra skills. So far they show no signs of interest in magical things. You always had an interest."

I nodded. I heard the door open to the doormroom and said, "Give my love to everyone. And Father," I smiled at him, "Thank you for this communication device. It may not tell my future, but at least I can always contact the most important parts of my past. My family."

"We love you, Darling. Call me anytime."

I turned to look at Maxine as I

wrapped the crystal ball in the velvet cloth. "You look like you've seen a ghost."

"I think I just did." She moved to her bed and dropped down on it. "I was on a walk and I saw what looked like my grandmother ahead of me, but younger and she was walking with several friends and they were giggling and laughing and pointing ahead of them. I couldn't see what was ahead of them, but the pack of girls broke off to go one direction and she stayed there. I thought she was waiting on me, but then... he came. And they ran into the forest and... I tried to follow, but as soon as I saw them kissing... poof! All gone."

"Wow." I took a seat on my bed. "That is some vision. What do you think it means?"

Maxine shook her head. "I have no idea, but he was not my grandfather. In fact, I'd seen his face before."

"Where?" I was practically holding my breath for this news.

"At Thurston's parent's house. It... really looked like a younger version of Thurston in the portrait. The first time I saw it, I mentioned to his brother how it seemed odd for him to be in uniform, but then I learned that was back in the days when the students wore uniforms. We don't anymore."

"So. Sounds like we may have a mystery to solve." I was hopeful of this distraction.

"Or it was a warning that someone in my family is already part of his family so if we hooked up we'd have little merchildren with fins on their foreheads shoving wands up their noses because they couldn't possibly understand magic." She flopped back onto the bed in such a dramatic fashion that I had to giggle. "Don't laugh at me."

We both laughed at that. "Well. There is only one way to find out."

She nodded. Either way, she needed to know.

CHAPTER TWENTY

A few months later…

Brazrothan

THIRST HAD GONE home for a weekend and that left me and my mate plenty of time and space to play in my room. I kept her sated, therefore, I kept the realm safe. It was a labor of love. A sacrifice I was willing to make for the good of the realm.

The rumors had become just that, myth, legend, whispers that could not be true because Eleanor Easternwind was a sweetheart and would never hurt anyone. She was a basic witch, not even first in her class, how could she possibly be the enemy of monsters?

"Do you want nachos?" she asked before conjuring up a plate for us both.

I laughed and nodded. "Love some."

"More than me?" she asked and pulled the plate in her hand out of my reach.

"I love nothing more than you." I winked at her. She was being a brat on purpose.

"What about Thirst?" she asked. "You're like brothers."

"We are brothers. By choice not biology, but he is my brother all the same." I nodded and she sat the nachos between us on the table.

"So… you know him really, really well." She dipped her chip into the cheese and looked up at me. My expression had to say it all. "I know it is obvious to you, me, and anyone paying attention, but they… belong together and she knows it. I think he knows it too."

I wasn't going to lie to her. "He doesn't want to know it. She dated his younger brother."

"Hmmm." She looked at me and I knew before she said anything. A plan was forming and I wasn't going to like it much. "What if we… gave them some… assistance? Just a little nudge."

"A little nudge?" I shook my head. I sighed and resigned to the fact that my mate wanted my help and while matchmaking was not my specialty, I would do whatever it took to make her happy. Even if it meant Thirst might try to murder me later. I laughed at the thought. She'd protect me. "What did you have in mind?"

She was such a monster. My monster and I loved her for that.

Thank you for reading this installation of the Blackthorn Academy for Supernaturals shared world!

Read the next book in the series now!

Watch for the other books in the Blackthorn Academy for Supernaturals shared world series.

Monster's Kiss

Monster's Delight

Monster's Spell

Monster's Enemy

Monster's Past

Monster's Secret

Monster's Savior

Monster's Reward

Monster's Obsession

Monster's Mayhem

Monster's Charm

Monster's Bride

and More!

Find more stories by Cara North at

creativewritingwithdrnagle.com

***

Signup to my newsletter and get a free copy of Cabin Fever

https://dl.bookfunnel.com/pr92gx0wx7

***

Read More from Cara North

creativewritingwithdrnagle.com

https://www.bookbub.com/authors/cara-north

https://www.facebook.com/caranorthauthor/

ABOUT CARA NORTH

Cara North is the long-time multiple-subgenre, romance pseudonym for Tonya Nagle, PhD. As a faculty member at multiple institutions of adult learning over the past twenty years, having a pen name was key to keeping her identities separate. Today, you can find everything under one website and additional pen names for YA and non-romance centric sci-fi and fantasy. She is a USMC veteran. She loves writing short stories for anthologies and connecting with her readers.

Made in the USA
Columbia, SC
22 March 2024

33174491R00127